To Ana ...,

Tales From Rainbow Bridge

Ian O'Neill and Friends

Published by New Generation Publishing in 2021

Copyright © Ian O'Neill 2021

First Edition

The author asserts the moral right under the Copyright, Designs and Patents Act 1988 to be identified as the author of this work.

All Rights reserved. No part of this publication may be reproduced, stored in a retrieval system or transmitted, in any form or by any means without the prior consent of the author, nor be otherwise circulated in any form of binding or cover other than that in which it is published and without a similar condition being imposed on the subsequent purchaser.

ISBN: 978-1-80369-077-3

www.newgeneration-publishing.com

New Generation Publishing

*To our heroes,
The dog wardens, rescuers, transporters, fosterers,
adopters, fundraisers, supporters and all who care ...
Thank-you.*

A big thank-you to Fay Done for the beautiful illustrations, and to my fellow writers, Jennifer Small, Caroline Byrne, Paula Harcombe, Marisa Piedade and Dave Gravestock for helping to create this wonderful book.

Foreword

I never imagined all those years ago when I drove up to Holyhead to pick up an elderly Golden Retriever, what that decision would lead to and just how much it would change my life. It was Boxing Day 2004 when I jumped into my car for the long drive to North Wales to pick up this old boy, whom I called Darcy. Together with my co-founders, Sandie (based in Ireland) and Pauline in the UK, we decided to form a dog rescue to help abandoned Golden Retrievers in Ireland to find their way to new families in England. Irish Retriever Rescue was born, and sixteen years later, is still helping Golden Retrievers to find their forever homes. It's been a long, and sometimes hard road, but a very satisfying one.

Today, with over a thousand dogs rescued, we have a network of drivers and fosterers, and a long list of adopters offering to take in these abandoned souls. We became a fully registered charity in 2013, but as ever, in common with all dog rescues, we are desperate for funds. So, when Ian, Caroline and Jennifer said that they were working on a book of short stories and poems about Rainbow Bridge, with the aim of raising funds for IRR, I was absolutely delighted. A big thank-you to all the contributors. It really is a wonderful book and one I think all dog lovers will love reading.

Lorraine Johnson, Co-founder and UK Co-ordinator, Autumn 2021

Tales from Rainbow Bridge

A Poem by Paula Harcombe

Do not be a shadow,
Of a memory left behind,
But bring joy and love and happiness,
And most of all peace of mind.

Some years ago I had a dream about my four Golden Retrievers: Sonny, Rory, Murphy, and Lucy. It was an incredibly special dream as at that time Sonny and Rory had both passed, and my current Goldens, Murphy and Lucy were playing with them in the snow. Many of my dreams are passive where I'm just observing but what struck me most about this one was that the dogs were speaking to each other.

When I woke the following morning I remembered it clearly and it left me feeling both sad and happy. The pain of losing a dog stays with you for ever. It lessens over time but it's always there. So, as much as I love dreaming about my first two boys it always leaves me with a deep longing the next day.

Over the following days a story began to come together, and I started to write down notes. The images were so clear in my mind that I was able to create a land. And this land was to become Rainbow Bridge. I wrote a story mainly for my own eyes although I did share it with some friends, and they liked it.

I didn't really think about it for another year or so. It was when a friend on a Golden Retriever group lost her dog in what can only be described as tragic circumstances, that the idea for a story came to me. Olly was just twenty months old when he died from a seizure and my friend and her family were absolutely devastated. I had watched Olly and his brother, Bennie, ever since their proud Mummy and

Daddy brought them home together as eight-week-old puppies from the breeder. Olly was a larger-than-life character who was always up to some mischief. His Mummy was often posting what he would get up to. But there was a clip that she posted of the two brothers chasing each other through a field of barley which stuck in my memory. It was typical Goldie play and was wonderful to see.

I thought about Olly a lot and I wondered about his journey to Rainbow Bridge and his story began to come together. The image from my dream was still clear in my head and I built the magical land around it. When I'd finished the story I sent it to my friend and waited anxiously while she read it. She loved it and said she found it very comforting to think of her little boy safe in a magical land.

We published it on the group and the reaction was overwhelming. I was quite surprised at the amount of positive feedback I received. It was an extremely sad story to write but the feedback was that they found great comfort in thinking of their dogs waiting for them on rainbow bridge.

I wrote further stories for friends who had lost their beloved dogs and received a similar reaction. The more stories I wrote the clearer Rainbow Bridge became to me. I described it to a special friend as if I was walking the hallowed turf myself and observing our dogs. That's when she called me the Chronicler, a name that is now commonly used amongst my readers.

We have talked about putting these stories into a book for a while but there never seemed to be the right time. So with the latest lockdown being announced at Christmas, Caroline suggested now was the perfect time to do it. So, here we are, Tales from Rainbow Bridge is born. I hope you enjoy it.

Ian O'Neill Spring 2021

Rainbow Bridge

A poem by Jennifer Small

What's that noise? It's Paddy and Murphy having forty winks –
I think they rather overdid the lunchtime drinks;
But they won't doze and snore for long, no fear
There's a delegation come to see them here.

There's Bonnie, Bailey, Bracken, Barley and Bella,
Angel and Abbey, Cooper, Cassie, Rosie and Ella,
Finlay and Flossie, Fergus, Lottie, Hector and Molly,
Milly & Tilly, Max, Roxy, Toby and Bess and Holly.

Old Gromit spoke for all the assembled crew –
As doyen of the Bridge it was his due –
'There's something that's preying on our mind,
We're worried about those we've left behind'.

'We need to tell our loved ones where we go
And of the land that lies under the rainbow.
Though we may be out of sight and far away,
They need to know we miss them every single day'.

With this sentiment Murphy could not disagree,
So, pen in claw, he composed this little homily;
'Pin back your ears' he woofed, 'and hark
To these words that I'm about to bark.

Errr! I'm Murphy O'Neill and here waiting his turn
Is my dear old mate, by name of Paddy Byrne,
We're the Rainbow Bridge's Welcome Committee
We're the first faces our new arrivals will see.

Do you wonder what happens to us when we're no more?
When you gently see us through that final door?
Do you think that we melt away into the shade?
A loving memory that will slowly fade?

Well, you really couldn't be more wrong!
Because we're never truly lost and gone.
And now we're here to tell you a story
Of a place filled with love, laughter and glory.

It's a land of endless joy and delight
Where Golden days flow gently into velvet night,
Where the sun shines and the skies are azure blue
And the rain falls softly like morning dew.

Our aches and pains and twinges are all gone
Sore and creaking joints have we none.
Old age and illness have quite passed us by
And on dancing paws across the grass we fly.

There are swampy bogs where we can roll
Ponds, streams and a delightful muddy hole;
And because our fur stays gleaming Golden clean
Baths are something few and far between!

We go to bed our tummies full and quite replete
Our dinner bowls always have the food we like to eat,
And when, worn out with play, on soft beds we sleep.
Curled up together, paw to paw, in a furry heap.

Though without you it can never truly be home
Don't fret that we're left sad and all alone;
There's always someone to lend a helping paw,
To comfort us when our hearts are sore.

Your prayers and love light us on our way
Over the Rainbow Bridge to a bright new day
And though we know how you grieve our loss
Don't fret, we'll be waiting when you come to cross.

From time to time from the Bridge we'll stream
To bring you comfort as you dream,
And though our spectral form you cannot see
You'll feel us as we lean once more against your knee.

We'll hear you as across the Bridge you slowly pace,
We'll never stop looking for your smiling face,
It's no matter if we're far away or very near
When you come at last, we'll be waiting for you here.

So when these tales you quietly sit and read
You'll see that for sadness there's no need
Think of us and keep us close-held in your heart
And then you'll know we'll never be apart.

Dear Reader, heed our Murphy's words so wise
And though our faithful friends are hid from our eyes,
On this one thing you may surely depend,
We'll meet again at the Rainbow's end.'

A Land of Magic

A Poem by Paula Harcombe

"In a field far away, (we know not where),
A magical elixir fills the air,
The pain is gone, the old feel young,
And sorrow turns to joy for each and everyone.

Dogs who struggled to move,
Can roll and gambol upside down,
And those who suffered pain,
No longer wear a frown.

To those who owned a dog once,
Please be rest assured,
Your pet is in a happy place,
Where sickness and pain are cured."

The Journey

A short story by Ian O'Neill

Mummy ...

I was surrounded by a swirling mist. A voice called out to me. 'Olly, follow the light.'

The words were barely whispered. I walked slowly forwards without knowing or purpose. The mist disorientated me.

'The light, Olly, follow the light.'

It was the voice again. I peered through the thick mist and could just about make out a shrouded light in the distance. Where was I?

'Keep moving towards the light Olly. One paw in front of the other.'

The faint echo of a woman's grieving tears stopped me momentarily. I turned around. *Mummy?*

The mist wrapped around me, suffocating, confusing, frightening. *Where am I?* The voice urged him on. 'Follow the light, Olly. Keep following the light.'

The voice was both comforting and reassuring. It soothed my fears. I kept walking. I sensed the mist was thinning. Or was it, hoped? The light became slowly brighter, my confidence grew, as did the purpose in my stride. I slowly emerged from the mist and found myself standing in front of a huge, shimmering golden arch. But I couldn't see anything through the archway other than a radiant, bright golden light.

'Welcome Olly.'

It was the voice again but now I could hear it clearly. I looked to my right to see a tall white horse standing across from the arch. My attention was drawn to the pointed horn protruding from its forehead.

'Are you a horse?'

It raised its head and smiled. 'Not a horse, Olly. I'm a Unicorn.' She lowered her head and pointed her long ivory horn at him as if to emphasise it. 'My name is Daetia.'

'Why am I here? Where's my Mummy, and Bennie and Bailey?'

Sadness clouded Daetia's ocean blue eyes. 'They are not here, Olly. This is a journey you will undertake without them.'

'But I thought my Mummy cared about me. She was always cuddling me and telling me how much she loved me.'

'Your Mummy loves you very much, Olly. She always will.'

I sat down and hung my head. I felt sad. 'I don't understand.'

Daetia walked over to me and lowered her head and kissed the soft fur on my ear. It felt nice. It was what my Mummy used to do. I felt the tears welling in my eyes.

'So young, Olly. So young to have to make this journey.'

I looked up at her, my eyes pleading. 'Tell me why I'm here, please.'

Daetia's kindly smile softened slightly as sadness tinged her eyes. 'You were terribly ill, Olly. Your Mummy and the Healers tried everything they possibly could to save you. But in the end, you were too weak. You are now on the next stage of your life journey. I am your guide, and will take you to Rainbow Bridge, a land of magic where you will be looked after.'

I felt desperately sad. I looked up at her through misty eyes. 'Will I see my family again?'

'I promise you, Olly, you will see all of your family again. One day they will make this very same journey and they will come for you.'

I turned around and looked into the mist. My old life lay back there somewhere. All the people and dogs I loved were on the other side of that mist. I momentarily thought about running back. I looked up into Daetia's kindly eyes and saw the love deep within them. I instinctively trusted her.

'Are you ready, Olly?'

I stood up and shook myself from head to tail. 'I'm

ready.'

Daetia smiled. 'Stand by my side, Olly. We will walk through the arch together.'

I walked over and stood by her side. I looked apprehensively through the arch and into the golden glow, then up at Daetia.

'There is nothing to fear, Olly. We are entering a land of love and magic.'

I stepped through the arch with Daetia by my side and we were instantly enveloped in the golden warmth. And within two steps we emerged into an emerald green meadow. Tall trees and brightly coloured flowery bushes lined its perimeter. Birds sang and butterflies fluttered around the bushes. A path led through the middle of the meadow towards the brow of a hill in the distance. A mild sun sat in the sky above me shedding its shallow light and warmth across the landscape. It looked and felt like paradise.

I studied my new surroundings in wonderment. 'But how?'

Daetia smiled warmly. It's magic, Olly. You have entered another world. Rainbow Bridge, your new home, is just the other side of that hill.'

I looked back towards the arch. 'I'm not far from my home and family.'

The Unicorn smiled again. 'You are only ever a thought away from them, Olly. You will never forget your family and they will never forget you, I promise. Come, my young friend, let's follow the path to the brow of the hill.'

I studied my surroundings as we walked. A welcome feeling of calmness swept over me as the fear dissipated. I'd always loved being out in the open and running free in the fields with my brothers. Oh how I was going to miss Bennie and Bailey.

A question popped into my head. I turned to Daetia. 'Where does magic come from?'

'Magic is everywhere, Olly, but not everyone sees it. Was it magical when you ran in the Fields of Gold with your brothers?'

I smiled at the memory and nodded. 'Oh yes.'

'The Faeries used their magic to create Rainbow Bridge. A place where all animals will be free from pain and fear; a place where they wait to be reunited with their loved ones. It truly is a land of beauty and wonderment, Olly.'

'But who will take me for walks and feed me?'

Daetia smiled again. 'The Elves will look after you and the Pixies will play with you.'

'Elves and Pixies?'

'They are creatures of Faery, Olly. Humans think they are fictional characters, but I can assure you that they are as real as you or me. In fact, it was the Elves who gave me my name, Daetia. It means white magic. And as for the Pixies, I think you will like them very much.'

As they approached the brow of the hill, Daetia stopped. She gazed down at Olly, and tears misted her eyes. 'This is where I leave you.'

My spirits dipped momentarily. 'But I thought you were taking me to Rainbow Bridge.'

'That is for another, Olly. My role is to bring you through the arch and into the magical land.'

'So who will take me the rest of the journey?'

'That will be me, young Olly,' said a voice from behind.

I turned to see what looked like a grown man walking towards me. 'Is he an Elf?'

'He is indeed, Olly. Let me introduce Baelon to you. He is the Guardian of Rainbow Bridge. He and his Elves will look after you now.'

Baelon knelt down and gently stroked my head and ears. I groaned softly as he did so, and happy memories stirred inside my head. I looked up into Baelon's kindly face and noticed his deep, brown, soulful eyes. I knew I could trust this Elf.

'Good day to you, young Olly,' said Baelon.

I did my best to smile but I felt sad at leaving Daetia. 'Will I see you again?'

She smiled reassuringly. 'I will always be with you,

Olly. I will be there when you need me the most.' She leant over and kissed his ear again. 'Now go with Baelon and embrace this wonderful new land.'

Baelon rubbed my head and ears again and said, 'Come Olly, let us walk together to your new home. A warm welcome awaits you, my young friend.'

I turned away with Baelon and walked by his side towards the brow of the hill. As I walked away from the Unicorn, I heard her whisper; 'Run free, sweet Olly.'

I trotted alongside Baelon taking in my new surroundings. There were some wonderful scents floating on the wind. Once on top of the hill we stopped and looked down into the valley below. My mouth dropped open as I gazed up in wonderment at the flower covered stone steps that rose high into the sky and over a deep blue lake. A rainbow straddled the bridge. To the left of the lake, dogs played on the grass in front of rows of thatched cottages. I thought it looked beautiful.

'Welcome to Rainbow Bridge, young Olly. This is your home now. Come, let us meet your new friends.'

As we walked down the hill, the dogs playing below noticed us and their play stopped. They began to form themselves into a long line, like a welcoming committee. The Golden Retrievers gathered in the middle. I felt a pang of anxiety deep down in my stomach.

'Relax young Olly,' reassured Baelon. 'They have all made the same journey as you my young friend. They will do their best to put you at your ease as they know how you feel at this precise moment.'

We stopped a few metres from the gathered pack. Baelon reached down and stroked my head and ears again. He turned to the assembled pack and addressed them directly. 'Please welcome our new young friend, Olly, to Rainbow Bridge.'

The pack immediately started barking and wagging their tails. The noise was deafening but all the dogs looked happy to see me. I wasn't sure how to react and looked to Baelon for reassurance.

'Go on, Olly, respond to them.'

I lifted my head and barked as loud as I could, my tail waving around and around like the sails of a windmill. It made me feel like my old self again. I felt good.

As the noise died down, two Goldens trotted up to him, tails swishing to and fro.

'Welcome, Olly, my name is Sonny-Boy, and this is my bro, Rory.' He turned to the assembled Goldens. 'This is Maisie and Zara, Rolo, Rio, Podge, Jake and Murphy, and Harry, Alfie and Chip, and Ziggy and Bonnie, and ...'

A Golden stood to the side and barked for their attention. 'Oh, I nearly forgot,' said Sonny, 'this is Bob. He likes to sing!'

He turned towards a Chocolate Labrador. 'And this is Toffee. She loves to play with us Goldens and sleeps in our cottage.'

My head was bursting with all the names, but I felt welcome and began to relax. They all seemed to want to talk to me.

'We can play all day if we want to,' said Rolo excitedly.

'And jump in muddy ponds and run through corn fields and nobody tells us off!' said Charlie as he danced on the spot.

'The Pixies are awesome,' said Chip. 'They will play all day if we want them to and they never tire of throwing a ball for us.'

'And they hide treats in the woods for us to find,' said Ziggy.

'And they're always playing tricks on us,' said Jake whose tail was wagging so fast that Olly thought he would take off.

'They are ace!' said Harry.

'And no matter how many times you tear your furry toys, there are always new ones to replace them,' said Murphy.

'The summer sun is bright but never too hot,' said Podge.

'And there are plenty of clear blue pools for us to swim in and cool down,' said Alfie.

'And best of all,' said Maisie, 'is that it always snows at Christmas, and it stays for as long as we want.'

'And we can play in the snow all day,' said Zara and Rio simultaneously.

Baelon knelt down by my side and playfully rubbed the fur around my neck. 'You see my young friend, there is much fun to be had on Rainbow Bridge. And you will never be ill again, no animal is ever ill here. You will have warmth when it's cold and can keep cool when it's hot. You will eat the food that you like the best. You will never want for anything Olly.'

I looked up at the Elf and said sadly, 'except my Mummy and my family.'

Baelon was momentarily lost for words. He placed his hand on Olly's chest over his heart. 'They are here, young Olly, and they always will be.'

I forced a smile. I sensed the other dogs felt the same as me. It was then the pack parted, and two distinctive looking Goldens walked through the middle of them. They stopped in front of me and said nothing for a moment.

I looked first at Baelon and then back at the two Goldens.

'My name is Toby, and this is Max. We're … we're your brothers, Olly.'

Toby and Max. I'd heard my Mummy talk about them many times. Their pictures were in our house. *My brothers ...*

'Don't worry little bro,' said Max stepping forward and nuzzling me. 'Toby and I will look after you.'

'Do you like running free in fields of tall barley, Olly?' asked Toby.

'I chased my brother Bennie through a golden field many times. We loved it more than anything.' I looked up to Baelon. 'Can I?'

'You can do whatever you so wish, young Olly. Run free through the golden fields with your brothers.'

Toby and Max stood protectively either side of me. The pack parted as the three of us trotted towards the hill out the back of the cottages. Then we broke into a run, three brothers side by side, our ears and tails flowing like sails in the wind. As we approached the golden fields, I slowed and watched as my two brothers disappeared into the tall barley. I stopped momentarily and looked to the far side of Rainbow Bridge to where the golden arch stood in the distance. Memories came flooding back to me through a mixture of tears and smiles. I was both happy and sad. I'd lost one family and found another. I couldn't wait for that day when we were all together again.

I whispered some words and allowed the gentle breeze to carry them home. 'It's goodbye for now, Mummy. The time we shared together was too short, but so special. I will carry those memories safely within my heart. Never forget me as I will never forget you. Until we meet again.'

I turned towards the Fields of Gold as the pack followed and together we charged into the tall barley to chase my brothers.

*

Lionpaws

A Short Story by Ian O'Neill

Rainbow Bridge was strangely subdued this night. A full moon rested majestic and proud over the flower covered stone bridge, casting its luminous white light all across the lake and beyond. Golden Retrievers sat outside their cottages quietly soaking in the atmosphere. All the usual suspects were there. Rory, Maisie, Zara, Charlie, Rolo, Bob, Rio, Murphy, Jake, Chip, Podge, Daisy, Bonnie, Ziggy, Harry, Alfie, Tilly, Toby and Max. Olly paced up and down. He didn't believe in wasting any waking moment by lying around.

'Come on, Max, come on Toby, let's have a chase around the lake? Or maybe a swim?'

'We've been playing all day,' said Toby wearily.

'Time to chill,' said Max, chin resting on his paws.

Olly sighed and lay down next to his brothers. 'Well, tomorrow then?'

Max and Toby smiled. 'Tomorrow will soon be here little bro.'

'I don't ever remember seeing a moon so beautiful and bright in all my years at the Bridge,' said Maisie gazing out across the meadow.

'I think it looks really pretty,' said Charlie, 'just like a Christmas scene. All we need is some snow.'

'I love Christmas,' said Daisy. 'My Mummy always bought me lots of presents. This will be my first Christmas away from her.' A look of sadness clouded her eyes.

Zara reached across and placed a tender paw on Daisy's shoulder. 'The first Christmas here is always the hardest. The Elves and Pixies really do try their best to make it happy for us. And we'll look after you.'

Sonny-Boy walked over from the cottages and looked up at the moon. 'I've never seen a moon like it before. It's like, it's like daylight.'

Toffee followed him and stopped a few metres away. 'It's what the Elves call a welcoming moon.'

Sonny sat down and watched Toffee as her nose twitched as she studied the sky. The dogs on the Bridge called her Toffee the Wise as she offered such insightful answers to their many questions. 'What is it Toffee? What is it you're feeling?'

Toffee's serious expression never wavered. She thought for a few moments before answering. 'Someone special approaches.'

Baelon suddenly emerged from one of the cottages and strode towards the brow of the hill. The arch to the human world was on the other side of the hill. It was a journey they had seen the Elf take many times. He momentarily hesitated and turned towards the Golden pack. He smiled enigmatically at them all and then said, 'He's coming.'

Baelon turned away from them and continued to stride up the hill.

Olly was immediately on his feet. 'Who's coming?' He trotted up to Sonny-Boy and Toffee. 'Who's Baelon talking about?'

'Someone very special,' said Toffee. She breathed slowly and thoughtfully for several seconds. 'He is a Golden legend. We should organise a special welcome for a dog of such stature.'

*

Baelon reached the brow of the hill just as Daetia stepped through the arch with her new arrival. It was immediately obvious to the Elf that this dog was indeed unique. He stood proud and tall alongside the Unicorn.

Daetia smiled at the Elf as he approached. 'Baelon, please welcome our new friend, Harvey.'

Baelon knelt down and stroked Harvey's head and ruff. 'Young Harvey, I'm not sure if you are the biggest Golden Retriever to come to Rainbow Bridge, but I am certain you are the curliest.'

Harvey held up one of his giant paws as if to shake Baelon's hand. The Elf took it in his right hand and shook it warmly. 'My Harvey, you have the paws of a Lion!'

Harvey smiled. 'I was known as Lionpaws by my Mummy's friends.'

Baelon laughed loudly. 'And they named you well! Come Lionpaws, Rainbow Bridge is waiting to welcome its special new friend.'

Harvey looked up at Daetia, his eyes sparkling with anticipation. 'My Mummy, she will be OK?'

Daetia lowered her head and kissed his ear. 'Your Mummy is grieving for you, Harvey, and she will be for a while. But the pain will slowly heal given time and she will be able to think of you and remember the wonderful times you shared. You have a bond between you that is unbreakable. Remember Harvey, you are only ever a dream away from each other. Now go with Baelon and embrace the next stage of your life journey.'

Baelon ruffled Harvey's curly coat and stood up and together they began the short walk up the hill as Daetia watched them. Harvey surveyed his new surroundings as they walked. The moonlight was so bright it illuminated the grass to an emerald glow. Harvey had never seen grass so lush and green. A sparkling array of jewelled stars smiled in the night-time sky.

Just before they reached the brow of the hill, Harvey hesitated for a moment. 'Baelon, I need to talk with you before I meet the other dogs.'

Baelon turned to Harvey, the moonlight reflecting in his kindly, dark eyes. 'What is it my friend?'

'I'm a little … I'm a little frightened.'

Baelon knelt down in front of Harvey and held his head in his hands. He looked deep into his eyes. 'Every dog that makes this journey is frightened, young Harvey. It is my job along with my Elf and Pixie family, to make sure you feel secure and have everything you need. The dogs waiting over that hill will become your friends. There is a bond between them all that is a joy to see.'

Harvey lowered his head momentarily. 'I've just left my best friend at home.'

Baelon sat down on the lush grass. 'Come, young Harvey, sit with me. We can talk a while.'

Harvey sat down next to Baelon and forced a smile. 'You keep calling me young. I'm fifteen years old.'

Baelon returned the smile. 'I am nearly two hundred years old. To me, at fifteen you are but a pup.'

Harvey liked the Elf as much as he liked the Unicorn. Kindness, love and understanding shone from them both. He felt comfortable being with them.

'I had a lovely Mummy. We shared everything together. We didn't have much need for anyone else. After my Daddy died suddenly eight years ago, she was heartbroken. We both were. We lost someone very special that day. I loved her so much. I loved her with all my heart. And when I thought I'd loved her as much as I could, I reached deep down inside myself and loved her even more.' Tears misted his eyes. 'It was hard to watch her struggle, but bit by bit she slowly rebuilt her life. Not the same as before but we had each other, and we were happy.'

'And then as I grew older, my body ached, and I could no longer walk far. The last two years were difficult. I kept falling over but my Mummy was always there and lifted me back up. I had what she called poopcidents. But she cleared up after me and never complained and always cuddled me afterwards. I felt loved, Baelon, I felt like I was the most loved dog in the world.'

The tears leaked freely from his eyes and dripped off the end of his nose. The Elf leant forward and cuddled Harvey just like his Mummy would have done. 'You are love, Harvey, that's what you do. You loved your Mummy through the most difficult time of her life; you loved her so much that when you needed more love and support at the end of your life, she was able to give it back and love you unconditionally in return.' Baelon dried Harvey's tears on his jacket sleeve. 'Your Mummy is going to grieve for you, Harvey, as you are going to grieve for her, but it is that love between you that is going to sustain you both. She will carry you in her heart alongside your Daddy and that is what will heal her.'

Harvey's heart ached for his Mummy but what the Elf said made sense. He had been ready for the next stage of his journey, but it was his love for his Mummy that kept him from leaving her. He did so for as long as could, and his Mummy knew that. But it was a testament to the depth of her love for him that she found the strength and courage to let him go.

He turned to Baelon and forced a smile. 'I'm ready.'

The Elf ruffled Harvey's curly ruff and climbed to his feet. Harvey stood up and together they walked those last few hundred metres to his new home, Rainbow Bridge. And when he reached the brow of the hill the view that greeted him nearly took his breath away. Flower covered stone steps, straddled by a rainbow, stretched high into the night sky. It looked magical.

But there was something else. Even his Elven companion looked amazed. A sea of dogs lined their route back towards the cottages where he would live. Golden Retrievers formed a guard of honour at the front of the huge pack. Every breed was there: German Shepherds, Rottweilers, Labradors, Dalmatians, Spaniels, Terriers, Collies, to name but a few, and of course the cross breeds.

Baelon looked confused, slightly bewildered even. 'In all my years at Rainbow Bridge, Harvey, I have never seen this. It is a welcome unlike anything I have ever witnessed before.'

The dogs stood quietly as a mark of respect for the new arrival and watched him intently. Harvey wasn't sure how to react. He turned to the Elf for guidance. Baelon looked back at him and shrugged his shoulders. 'Let us meet your Golden friends, Harvey.'

They took tentative steps down the hill towards the cottages and there was a mighty howl from the back of the canine throng, which was met with an equally vociferous howl from the other side of the massive pack. As Harvey walked alongside Baelon he held his head up high and walked as confidently as he could, as isolated howls echoed around the hillside.

'My legs and back no longer hurt,' whispered Harvey.

'It's the magic of the Bridge,' said Baelon. 'Your health is returned, Harvey; you have the body of a young dog again but with the wisdom of an older one.'

The howls rang all around Harvey now as he neared the Goldens waiting in front of the cottages. He'd never experienced anything like it, and he most certainly had never felt exhilaration like it before in his entire life. The pride he felt at that moment ran from the tip of his nose to the end of his tail. As he walked in between the lines of Goldens they fell in behind him. He looked like a majestic King parading before his subjects.

Harvey and Baelon stopped a few metres from the waiting Goldens assembled in front of the cottages. Baelon raised his hand to ask for quiet from the howling dogs on the hill. He stood tall and breathed deeply.

'Rainbow Bridge, please welcome our new friend, Harvey, who is also known as Lionpaws.'

Every dog held their heads back and barked as loud as they could. Some stood up on their hind legs barking their welcome to Harvey. Rainbow Bridge resonated with the love and respect that they felt for the curly one. It was a recognition that he was indeed a legend of the Golden Retriever breed. The noise was deafening and went on for several minutes until Baelon raised his right arm again.

Once quiet had resumed, Sonny-Boy stepped forward and stood directly in front of Harvey. He lifted his right paw and placed it on Harvey's left shoulder and placed his head on his other shoulder and nuzzled him. It was a Rainbow Bridge welcome and Harvey responded in kind. Sonny stepped back and studied the huge, curly boy who stood in front of him. He turned to Rory and said, 'Well, bro, you are no longer the curliest Golden on Rainbow Bridge.' Rory smiled and barked his approval. 'Welcome, Harvey, my name is Sonny-Boy, and these are my Golden friends. You will get to meet them all over the coming days.'

Harvey looked along the line of Golden Retrievers stood in front of him. This was familiar territory as he and his Mummy had spent many happy hours at Golden gatherings. He looked over his shoulder, dogs covered the whole of the hill that led back to the arch. It was a sight to gladden any heart. Harvey felt humbled that they would turn out for him. He barked nervously in acknowledgement of the amazing welcome he'd just had.

'Thank-you for such a warm welcome. I'm not sure what I've done to receive such an honour, but I thank you all from the bottom of my heart.'

Toffee stepped forward and nuzzled Harvey just like Sonny had done. 'You embody love and kindness, Harvey, and you have the rare gift of healing others. Rainbow Bridge welcomes and embraces you.'

Olly could no longer contain his excitement and bounded forward, his tail wagging furiously as usual. 'Why do they call you Lionpaws?'

Harvey held up his giant right front paw. 'Give me your paw young fella.'

Olly did as he asked and watched his front paw disappear into Harvey's. 'Wow! You're a giant!'

'Hardly,' laughed Harvey, 'but according to my Mummy's hooman friends, I am the curliest Golden Retriever in the world. They call me Curlywurlycuddlebumptious.'

Olly barked his laughter. 'What an awesome nickname! My name is Olly and I love to run through the Fields of Gold with my brothers and my friends. Do you Harvey?'

'It's been a while since I've done that, young Olly,' said Harvey.

Olly looked up at Baelon expectantly. 'Can we?'

'You can do whatsoever you wish.' He turned to Harvey. 'Go with him, in fact, go with them all and run free Lionpaws, just like you did as a young dog.'

The Goldie pack burst into spontaneous barking and surrounded Harvey. He stepped forward and stood alongside Olly. 'Well, young fella, you'd better show me the way.'

Olly and Harvey led the pack away from the cottages and towards the golden fields in the distance. They broke into a trot before running fast and free. Harvey felt like a young dog again, energy surging along the entire length of his body, no aches or pains slowing him and the wind blowing through his curly coat and his tail held high and proud like a sail.

The running pack spread like a Golden wave across the grass as they approached the fields of barley. Baelon, the Elf, looked on with pride. It was a sight that made his heart sing. *Is there anything better?* he thought.

Harvey slowed as he approached the barley and allowed the Golden pack to run past him. He looked back towards the arch that led to the human world. So many thoughts crowded his mind, and the tears misted his eyes again.

'Never forget me, Mummy, as I will never forget you.' He whispered the words and let the breeze carry them home to her. 'And remember, I am only ever a dream away.'

He turned into the fields of tall barley and ran with the Goldens just as he did as a young dog. Harvey Lionpaws, Golden Retriever, Curlywurlycuddlebumptious, live forever ...

*

Cody

A Short Story by Ian O'Neill

Daetia anxiously paced up and down in front of the golden arch. She was awaiting her latest arrival and periodically peered into the swirling mist between the worlds. She was a Unicorn; she straddled time; she was eternal, a creature of Faery. She was magic. But today all of her emotions would be familiar to any grieving human. She felt so sad that tears streamed from her eyes.

Daetia spent her life in between the worlds and didn't profess to understand either in any great depth. But she understood grief. The anguished tears of the grieving parents could sometimes be heard through the mist and would have a profound effect on her. Her job, if that's how you would describe what she did, was to offer comfort and love to the dogs when they arrived at the arch. Dogs that were leaving the beloved and familiar behind them. It was a job that she loved but at times it drained her. Even creatures of Faery suffered from the emotional distress of loss.

Then she heard it. Sweet celestial music drifted through the mist. It sounded like a choir of angels. Her tears now flowed freely. She looked into the mist and saw a tall, shadowy figure slowly approaching her. A beautiful lady with long, flowing blonde hair hanging loosely over a snow-white full-length gown, gradually emerged from the mist. Two arched golden wings on her back showed that she was an angel. In her arms she cradled a tiny, lifeless puppy.

She stopped in front of Daetia and smiled warmly. The Unicorn felt an overwhelming sense of love wash over her. Daetia leant forward and gently kissed the puppy on his head and watched as her healing tears bathed him. She stepped back and the angel held the puppy close to her breast before holding him out to Daetia. The puppy started to wriggle and emitted tiny squeaks and squeals that made her heart sing. His eyes opened and he looked up at the angel and Daetia in wonderment.

Daetia looked at him adoringly and said, 'Welcome to Rainbow Bridge, Cody, your forever home.'

The angel joined Daetia and together they stepped through the arch, emerging onto the lush green grass of Rainbow Bridge. The familiar scene of bright, colourful flowers and shrubbery bathed in soothing sunshine greeted them. Baelon the Elf was already waiting. His dark eyes glistened with happy tears as he saw the wriggling puppy cradled in the angel's arms. She slowly walked over to him and held out the puppy. Baelon took the precious Golden boy and hugged him tenderly to his breast.

'Welcome little Cody. May Rainbow Bridge nourish and heal you.'

The angel cupped Baelon's face in her hands and tenderly kissed his cheek. Then she leant over and kissed Cody's tiny little nose. She turned to Daetia and embraced her before walking back through the golden arch.

Daetia stepped forward and took one more look at Cody. She looked lovingly at Baelon and said, 'He is just so beautiful.'

'He's perfect,' said Baelon. 'Now I must get him to the cottage where his milk is warming. Look after yourself, Daetia, and rest assured that young Cody will get the very best of care from our Healers.'

Baelon walked up the hill at a brisk pace but hesitated once he reached the top. He held up Cody underneath the shadow of the stone bridge and said, 'Look my young friend, your new home. It is a land of magic and beauty and I make you this promise that you will never want for anything. Health, food, warmth, friendship and love will be yours forever. You are about to join the most wonderful, loyal Golden family a young dog could ever wish for. Come, my young friend, it is time to meet them.'

Baelon strode purposefully towards the cottages and the Goldens resting outside ran over as soon as they saw him approaching. Every journey he made to the arch always meant a new arrival, so they had to welcome them in true Goldie style.

'What's their name? What happened to them? Oh so tiny. Oh bless.' The questions continued to rain on the Elf. He held up his hand and said, 'Let's get our young friend inside the cottage and settled. Then we must feed him warm milk and let him rest.'

Baelon walked the last few steps to the cottages surrounded by a Golden pack. Young Cody sniffed the air all around him. If he couldn't see them, he could sense them. Their love covered him like a warm Golden blanket. The Elf climbed the steps and took Cody in through the open door and over to a large bed in the corner, where Maisie lay with another tiny puppy snuggling against her tummy.

Baelon hesitated for a moment and took in the beautiful scene, before kneeling down in front of Maisie. He held out the precious puppy to her and said, 'Let me introduce you to Cody. He is Bambi's brother.'

Her face lit up and tears misted her eyes. 'Oh Baelon, he is absolutely beautiful.'

Baelon placed Cody next to his sister against Maisie's tummy. Cody snuggled into his sister and wriggled and squeaked in tune with her. Maisie gazed at them like any proud mother admiring her puppies.

'What happened to the poor little soul?' she asked.

'It was not meant to be, Maisie. Like his sister he was too frail to survive in the human world, but the magic of Rainbow Bridge will heal them both, along with your Golden love, of course.'

A tall Aelf (female Elf) walked into the cottage holding two small bottles of milk with teats fitted.

'Charnor, your timing is perfect. I think our two young friends are ready to feed,' said Baelon stepping out of the way.

'Not before I've cleaned Cody,' said Maisie, and proceeded to lick his face, ears, eyes and tummy just like any Golden Mummy. 'Now you can feed them,' smiled Maisie, her work complete.

Charnor knelt down and placed the teat by Bambi's mouth, and she immediately took it and sucked the warm milk through. She held the other up to Cody and he hesitated. She saw the concern on Baelon's face. 'Don't look so worried my friend, it's new to him. He will soon learn as his sister did to take the milk.' And he did, closing his little mouth around the teat and sucking the milk through and making the same contented noises as Bambi.

'You have the Healer's calm assurance, Charnor,' smiled Baelon. 'I will leave you to your work.'

He turned around to see a Golden semi-circle of female retrievers sat watching the beautiful scene unfold in front of them. Zara, Zoe, Roxy, Hannah, Bonnie, Honey, Annie, Meggie, Molly, Millie, Ava, Willow, Megan, Misty, Maggie, Daisy, Martha, Ivy, Maddie, Suzie, Katie, Amy, Candy, Erin and Holly, looked on adoringly as the two Golden babies fed and wriggled on Maisie's tummy. He discreetly stepped through them and out of the door, hesitating for a second to look back and take in the wonderful scene for one more precious moment.

'How wonderful is that?'

Baelon looked down to see Harvey sitting by his side watching Maisie with the puppies. He knelt down beside him and placed his arm around the curly one's body and kissed his head. 'It's what we are about, Harvey. We love and look after each other. And that's how I hope it will always be, my young friend.'

*

Six Months Later

As the sun set over Rainbow Bridge casting its soft, gentle glow across the landscape, two Golden Retrievers emerged from the barley. They hesitated as they looked across the crystal blue lake, admiring the stunning view laid out before them. They both stood erect and proud, their fine heads held high, pink tongues hanging out the sides of their mouths and fan tails standing upright in the gentle breeze like golden sails.

The magic of Rainbow Bridge is beyond question, but there is something else that defines that special place. And that is the unconditional and pure love that the animals share with each other. Magic is magical and love is universal, and Bambi and Cody standing there is testament to both.

Something I have learned through writing these stories is that our Golden children never die. Once they enter our lives, our consciousness, they embed themselves in our hearts and that's where they stay. Rainbow Bridge is that special place we hold them in until that moment our own mortality comes to an end and we are once again reunited with our precious Golden babies.

*

Little Sausage

A Short Story by Ian O'Neill

Baelon stood on top of the hill looking down onto the peaceful cottages. He held the precious puppy close to his chest as he wriggled in his arms. The angels and Daetia had worked a miracle once again. Another puppy was saved.

It was the middle of the night and Rainbow Bridge slept. All of the dogs were tucked up safely in their beds and at rest. Sleep was a rare luxury when you were the Guardian of Rainbow Bridge, but it was a small price to pay for Baelon. He loved his job with every ounce of his being. And as he held that precious puppy in his arms he thought his heart would burst with joy. Tears misted his eyes as he looked around that magical place. Rainbow Bridge, where all dogs came to be safe and happy as they waited for their mummies and daddies.

Baelon kissed the puppy on his head and whispered, 'Come, Little Sausage, let's introduce you to your new Mummy and family.'

He strode purposefully down the hill towards the nearest cottage. He opened the door and crept silently inside, stepping carefully around the sleeping dogs. He stopped in front of Maisie and watched her as she peacefully slept. Cody to one side of her and Bambi to the other. Tears once again filled his eyes and he knelt down beside her and whispered, 'Maisie', close to her ear.

She opened her eyes and looked up at him. 'Baelon? Is everything OK?'

He held up his precious bundle to her and her face melted into tears. 'Oh Baelon. He's beautiful.' She sat up and kissed the little puppy on his nose. 'Does he have a name?'

A broad smile spread across the Elf's face. 'Little Sausage, he is only days old.'

Maisie lay back down on her bed and said, 'Please let him snuggle into me. I will clean him while you fetch some milk.'

The Elf gently placed him next to Maisie in her bed and carefully stepped back through the dogs. Maisie looked down on the sleeping puppy and bathed him in her tears. 'Hello Little Sausage, I'm your new Mummy.'

Cody stirred next to her and lifted his head. 'Mummy Maisie, I'm frightened.'

She reached across and gently stroked his head with her paw. 'Don't worry, little one, it's just a bad dream.'

Cody rubbed his eyes with his paws and sat up. He saw the puppy sleeping next to Maisie.

'He's your new little brother,' she smiled.

Cody watched the wriggling puppy as Maisie washed him with her tongue. He looked sad. 'Does that mean you won't be my Mummy anymore?'

She leant across and kissed his head. 'Of course not. I'll always be Mummy to you and Bambi, but this little one needs a Mummy too. We have enough love between us to share with him.'

Cody stood up and leant over the puppy and sniffed him. 'He's lovely, Mummy Maisie. What's his name?'

She finished cleaning him and said, 'Little Sausage.'

Cody smiled and licked the puppy's nose. He turned to Maisie and said, 'I love him Mummy Maisie …'

*

Murphy's Dream

A Short Story by Ian O'Neill

The three Golden pals ran through the fields with an intent and a purpose that was only apparent to them. What where they chasing? Probably nothing, but it didn't matter. They ran, sometimes side by side, sometimes in single file, but they ran. Their tails stretched out behind them like fan sails; their ears waving in the wind. A sight that many of us have seen a thousand times but one that never loses, either its appeal, or joy.

They continued their run until they reached a deep stream and then, one by one, they took a leap of faith and came splashing down in the water. Chaos ensued as they thrashed about chasing each other and jumping on top of one another. It was Goldie play at its best. And when they were ready, they climbed out of the stream, shook off the excess water from their coats and then collapsed onto the grass.

'That was awesome,' said Murphy. 'I needed that.'

'We always love a run, don't we bro,' said Sonny.

'We sure do,' said Rory.

Murphy sat up and looked around their surroundings. They were in the middle of a lush green meadow that stretched for as far as the eye could see. The stream whispered to them as it carved its way through the meadow. Clumps of weeping willows rested their drooping branches in the clear, running water. A cold, crisp, early winter's sunny day made it near perfection. A day to make your heart sing and the three friends' hearts sang in unison.

Murphy turned to his two pals and smiled. 'I love running with you two. You never ask questions; I can just be with you.'

'We're mates,' said Rory. 'That's what mates do.'

'But it's like you understand me. Sometimes I just need to get away and I have to run and run. Thoughts crowd my head and feelings overwhelm me, it's the only way to get rid of them.'

'Nothing better than a run and swim,' agreed Sonny. 'Then back to the cottage for a grand supper.'

'The best,' agreed Murphy.

They sat quietly for several minutes, just enjoying their surroundings. The sound of the running water soothed Murphy's frayed emotions. He had many friends on the Bridge, but Sonny and Rory were his closest and he would often confide in them. They felt like brothers to him. He had something on his mind, and he needed to share it.

'Are you two able to go back home to see your Mummy and Daddy?'

Sonny looked quizzically at him. 'I'm not sure what you mean.'

'I hear the others talking about how they can think about home before they go to sleep then visit their mummies and daddies in their dreams. Olly often talks about it. I would love to but no matter how hard I try it never happens.'

'We often think of home,' said Sonny. 'We are fortunate that, being brothers, we can talk about our parents, where we used to live and the fields we ran in. We can reach back in our imaginations and it seems real to us both.'

'Sometimes when we talk about home our Daddy comes to see us,' said Rory.

'He comes here to Rainbow Bridge?' said Murphy.

'It seems like a dream,' said Sonny. 'But we walk with him.'

Murphy looked enviously at them. 'Oh I wish my Mummy could come and walk with me.'

Sonny and Rory smiled sympathetically. 'I'm sure it will happen one day, my friend, probably when you least expect it,' said Sonny.

A gong sounded in the far distance. 'Supper time,' said Rory jumping to his feet. 'Chicken, rice and vegetables tonight. Come on boys!'

And the three pals ran off together across the meadow, back towards their cottages.

*

Murphy woke in the middle of the night and looked around him. He was surrounded by sleeping Goldies. An open log fire burned in the grate across from him. It was a peaceful scene but for some reason Murphy didn't feel sleepy. He stood up, stretched and walked over to the water bowl and took a long drink. Water dripped from his mouth onto the floor as he walked in and out of the beds. He needed some fresh air so pushed the door open and stepped out into the night.

He sat on the veranda and looked up into a star-filled sky. A full moon sat overlooking the stone bridge shedding a comforting glow across the landscape. Murphy thought it looked beautiful. He walked out onto the lush grass head held high, his nose twitching as he sensed all of the amazing smells riding on the night-time breeze. He was about to turn around and go back into the cottage when he suddenly caught a familiar scent.

It obviously conjured happy memories as it made him feel good. He peered out into the shadows, his nose continuing to twitch, looking for the source of the beautiful scent. In the distance he could see a person slowly walking towards him. Something deep inside of him stirred as his heart fluttered. He knew this person; he recognised the walk. He stood and his tail started to wag in anticipation. He took a few tentative steps forward, constantly peering into the night gloom.

A woman emerged from the shadows, stopped and looked at him. A huge smile spread across her lips as tears trickled slowly down her face. She knelt down and opened her arms wide. Her soft, gentle voice called out, 'Murph.'

He hesitated. Were his senses playing tricks with him? It couldn't be, could it? The smile that had melted his heart a thousand times before, slowly spread across her face and he knew. 'Mummy!' He sprang forward and almost dived into her arms. She held him tightly, both laughing and crying at the same time. 'My Mummy!'

'Oh darling, Murph, I've missed you.'

Murphy kissed her face and threw his paws around her shoulders. They sat quietly embracing each other for what, to them, seemed like forever but was only a brief moment in time. He took a step back from her and looked at her in wonderment. 'Mummy! Is it really you?'

'Yes it is, my special boy.'

Murphy suddenly looked troubled. 'Mummy, you're not …?'

'No, I'm fine, I promise you.'

'But how are you able to be here? I …'

She pulled him to her and hugged him again, kissing his shiny black nose. 'I asked my friend to look out for you. He found you and here I am.'

Murphy looked puzzled. 'Do you know Baelon the Elf? Or Daetia the Unicorn?'

She shook her head. 'No, my darling. My friend is the Chronicler of Rainbow Bridge.'

Murphy sat back in shocked silence. His Mummy knew the Chronicler. 'My friends often talk about him. Nobody has seen him; we weren't even sure if he really exists.'

'Oh, he is real my precious boy. I have met him many times. Everybody knows him, but nobody knows him. He writes about Rainbow Bridge and all the wonderful dogs here.'

Murphy snuggled up to his Mummy again and she wrapped her arms around his soft furry body. She sighed, 'Oh Murphy, I have missed you so much my beautiful boy.'

Murphy snuggled into her as close as he could, and they sat hugging each other in the mellow moonlight. Murphy suddenly pulled away. 'Mummy, let me take you around the lake. It's beautiful. It will be just like the old times when we walked together.'

She climbed to her feet and the two of them walked side by side towards the lake, under the shadow of the huge stone bridge. She looked up and marvelled at the stone steps that towered above her.

'Mummy? Can I ask you a question?'

'Of course,' she smiled.

'Do you think the steps lead up to Heaven?'

She followed the flower covered steps with her eyes as they disappeared within the stars of the dark night-time sky. It was impossible to convey the mystery of the stone structure in mere words. It was truly magical.

'The honest answer is I don't know. But what I do know is that one day your daddy, me, you and all of your brothers and sisters will climb those stone steps together, and that my precious boy, is the most important thing.'

Murphy cuddled up to her and kissed her hand. 'I'll go anywhere as long as it's with you, Mummy.'

Tears glistened her eyes again as she ruffled his ears. They continued around the lake until they came across a wooden bench. 'This is where the Elves sit, Mummy, when they're watching us play in the lake. Shall we sit here together?'

She sat down and Murphy jumped up on the bench next to her and rested his head on her shoulder. She wrapped her arms around him, and whispered, 'oh Murph, it's been so long since I held you like this.'

He kissed her cheek and rested his head against her. 'Can we stay here forever, Mummy?'

'Oh I wish, my beautiful boy, I wish …'

They sat quietly for a while just being with each other. No words were spoken, no words were needed. Murphy's anxieties all disappeared within his Mummy's hug. His mind was empty of thoughts; he was at peace.

She reached into her pocket. 'I have something for you.' She held it up to him. It was a collar pendant. There was an inscription in italics written on it. *For my beautiful Murphy, always loved, always remembered, always missed, Mummy xxx*

Tears misted his eyes. 'Oh Mummy, that is beautiful.'

'Here, let me clip it onto your collar.' She carefully attached it to the metal ring on his collar. 'There you are my beautiful boy. Something to touch with your paw when you're missing me.'

Murphy kissed her cheek. 'Oh I will, Mummy.' He rested his head on her shoulder as she wrapped her arms around him and they both drifted off into a deep and peaceful sleep.'

*

'Come on sleepy head, it's way past breakfast time.'

Murphy looked up into the smiling face of Baelon. He lazily lifted his head and rubbed his eyes with his paws. 'Why didn't you wake me earlier?'

'You looked so peaceful that Sonny and Rory said to let you rest. They're out by the lake waiting for you. I've kept you some porridge.' Baelon placed a bowl next to Murphy's bed. He got up, stretched his body and shook his head. He devoured the porridge in seconds, took a healthy drink of water and trotted out onto the veranda and sat down next to Baelon as he watched the dogs play on the grass.

'I had the most amazing dream last night, Baelon.'

The Elf smiled and ruffled his head. 'I'm pleased for you, Murphy. Dreams are good for us, especially happy ones.'

'Oh Baelon, this was the best. My Mummy came to see me.'

Baelon gave him a warm hug. 'They are dreams that lift us.'

Murphy stood up and shook his head again, but this time his collar made a jingling sound. Baelon reached to his collar and held something in his hand. 'What is this, my young friend?' He leant over and studied it. He looked at Murphy, smiled warmly, and said, 'it has an inscription.' And then he read it; 'For my beautiful Murphy, always loved, always remembered, always missed, Mummy xxx.'

*

The Abused and the Abandoned

A short story by Jennifer Small

It was a beautiful, sunny day at Rainbow Bridge. All the dogs were out of their cottages; some were splashing in the bubbling stream, some were playing 'chase'; some were snoozing quietly with the soft breeze ruffling their fur while others lay on their backs warming their tummies in the sun.

Well, almost all. Some way off three Retrievers sat in a silent little group, their backs turned towards their friends. Nestled between their furry paws were three tiny puppies. The dogs were Decca, Marcus and Laurie, but these were not, of course, the names by which they went in the other world – those names reminded them so much of the misery and unhappiness of their former existence that, when they came to the Bridge, Baelon had told them to choose brand-new names to start their brand-new lives. And so they became Decca, Marcus and Laurie. The pups had no names at all.

They were talking quietly together sharing with each other the stories of their lives. Marcus had offered to tell his tale first.

'I was bought as a Christmas present for the children,' he said. 'At first they made a great fuss of me and they seemed to love me but after a few months they grew tired of me. They said that I was noisy, that I barked too much and that I brought mud into the house. Nobody wanted to walk me or feed me or brush me, so they decided to rehome me, and they offered me 'free to a good home'. A lady came to see me; she seemed nice, she stroked me, and she told my humans that I would be cherished and cared for, so they just gave me away. She took me to her car and put me inside; I tried to lick her hand to show how grateful I was, but she shouted at me and hit me with a stick. I was so shocked that I just curled up in a corner and kept quiet. Soon we came to a big barn-like building. She pulled me out of the car and took me inside; there was a big ring in the centre of the barn with lots of sawdust. A man came up and he grabbed hold of me, and he tied my front feet tightly together and then wrapped tape around my muzzle so I couldn't walk or open my mouth. I was so afraid – what was happening? Then he threw me into the ring and out of nowhere four big fierce dogs jumped on me. They were growling and snarling and foaming at the jaws, and they started to bite me; they ripped my ears and bit my face and tore my legs and body apart. I couldn't run away or fight – I didn't know how to fight anyway – I'm a Retriever and we are made to love not to fight. There were men standing around and I wondered why no one came to help me, but they were all laughing and shouting, 'Bait! Bait!' It was then that I realized that there would be no rescue for me, there was no loving new home waiting for me and that my life would end here in dreadful pain and misery in front of a jeering braying mob. I would die not understanding why anyone would want to hurt me like this. When I couldn't stand up anymore, the man called the dogs off and picked me up and threw me into the back of his van. I hurt so much, and I was bleeding so badly. He drove me into the country and threw me into a deep muddy ditch by the side of the road. I think that I must have died there because the next thing that I knew, I was here and Daetia was blowing gently on my wounds and helping to heal them.'

Decca and Laurie were silent hardly able to believe that anyone could be so cruel.

'I was bought as a present too' said Laurie 'and like you, my people soon couldn't be bothered with me. I wasn't allowed into the house and I was chained up in a concrete yard all day and night. No-one came to talk to me and often they forgot to feed me, so I was always hungry and got very thin. I was caked in filth and smelled dreadful; I hated it but what could I do? I was chained up and couldn't move more than a few feet. Sometimes the children would poke me with sharp sticks or throw stones at me to hear me yelp in pain or they'd put my water-bowl out of reach so I couldn't drink.

I did have a kennel once with a piece of cardboard in it to sleep on, but the cardboard got wet and disintegrated and no-one replaced it, so I slept on the cold wooden boards. Then the kennel fell apart and no-one repaired it, so I had to sleep out in the open on the freezing concrete in all weather. One winter it was very cold, and it started to sleet. I was soaked through and my fur started to freeze – I couldn't stop shaking! Then it began to snow, and I thought that surely someone would let me have some shelter. I didn't expect to be let into the house, but I could have curled up in the porch. No-one came so I barked to remind them that I was still outside. My master came to the door; he swore at me and threw a brick at me. It hit me and I must have howled because he came out and started to kick me with his heavy boots. I felt my ribs splinter and break, and I started to cry but he just kicked me again and again and slammed the door shut. There was no shelter, so I curled in a tight ball up shivering and whimpering in pain on the concrete on the end of my chain. At first I was so, so cold and then it was like a miracle! I didn't feel so cold anymore and the thick snow covered me like a warm blanket. It got thicker and thicker until I was completely buried and then I don't remember anything until I woke up in the sunshine here with Daetia gently nuzzling me and helping me to my feet. I think that I died there under the snow'.

A tear ran down Decca's snout as she listened. 'What happened to you, Decca?' asked Marcus.

'I had a family for many years,' sighed Decca. 'I thought that they loved me; we went for walks, they stroked and patted me, we went on holiday together and they took me to nice places in the car. One day we went for a car ride and we stopped by the side of a busy road – I thought that it was for me to stretch my legs because I was getting old and a bit stiff by then. I jumped out of the car and went to sniff some grass and to my surprise, my master got back in, slammed the door and drove off leaving me by the side of the road. I thought that he must have thought that I had jumped back in the car and that when he realised his mistake, he'd come back for me, so I waited. I waited for two days but he never came back. I was in despair but eventually a van came and collected me; it didn't take me home though but to a place called 'Pound' where I was put in a cold bare kennel. They weren't cruel to me, but I was confused, sad and lonely. What had I done for my family to abandon me by the roadside? I thought that I'd been a good, faithful, loving dog but I must have done something very wrong for them not to want me anymore. After a few days I heard someone say, 'She's too old, no-one's going to come for her – her time's up,' and I realized that they were talking about me! A man came to my kennel and he said 'Sorry, old girl – you've run out of time,' and he put a needle in my leg and left me. I just fell asleep – it didn't hurt but I knew that I was dying alone and unwanted with no-one to hold me and comfort me in my last moments and that made me very sad. I never did find out why my family abandoned me, but I think it was just because I grew old'.

All through the stories, the puppies had been silent. Aren't you going to tell us your story?' asked Marcus.

'We don't really have one' said the oldest, largest puppy. 'We remember being with our Mummy in a cage; it wasn't very clean or comfortable, but we were very small, only just born really, and we loved our Mummy so much. It was bliss being snuggled up in her warm fur as she fed and cleaned us, but it didn't last. One day a man came in and looked at us and said, 'They're no good – runts, all of them,' and he picked us up and pushed us into a smelly dark sack. We started to cry and tried to scrabble out, but he tied the sack up; we huddled together, whimpering for our Mummy and we could hear her crying for us, but she couldn't save us. The next thing we knew we were flying through the air in the sack into icy-cold water; we tried to bark so someone would rescue us, but we were so little that we made hardly any noise and as we opened our mouths freezing water rushed in and we couldn't breathe anymore. Then we woke up here and Daetia was lying down next to us covering us with her silky white mane to keep us warm.'

'I don't know how we could have done anything wrong,' piped up the smallest puppy, 'we hadn't even quite got our eyes open, and we hadn't left our Mummy's side. It must have been because we aren't any good – runts like the man said.'

'You are not runts!' exclaimed Decca. 'You are absolutely perfect and don't let anyone tell you otherwise!'

'What's going to happen to us now? asked Laurie. 'All the dogs here are waiting for their Mummies and Daddies to come and go over the Bridge with them. We don't have anybody to come for us'.

They sat and thought about this for a while. Then Marcus stood up and said 'I know! We'll go and ask Baelon – he'll be able to help us!' So they set off to find Baelon. The puppies were too small to keep up with Marcus, Laurie and Decca so they each took one in their mouths and gently carried them along.

Baelon was sitting with his back against a sun-warmed stone enjoying some well-earned rest when he saw the little party approach. 'Hello, my children,' he greeted them, 'what a delegation and so serious! You look troubled. What can I do for you?'

They put the puppies down carefully at Baelon's feet and Marcus, who had agreed to act as spokesman, said, 'We are very worried, Baelon. Everyone here is waiting for their loved ones to come under the Rainbow so they can all go over the Bridge together. We have no-one to wait for, no-one loved, wanted or cared for us and we have no-one to take us across the Bridge. What will happen to us?'

Baelon smiled. 'Of course you have someone to take you across the Bridge, someone very, very special. When the time is right, you will meet a wonderful person called a Rescuer, someone who has devoted their life to caring for lost, hurt and abandoned dogs and they will come just for you'.

'How will we know who that is?' asked Decca, 'we've never seen a Rescuer'.

'They will come under the Rainbow,' replied Baelon,

'and kneel down in the grass, call your names out loud and open their arms wide to gather you into their heart. Then they will take you across the Bridge.'

Marcus, Laurie and Decca smiled and woofed with joy and relief, but the puppies were strangely silent. 'Excuse me,' the largest one said, 'but what about us? The Rescuer won't know who we are and won't be able to call us – we were too young and unimportant to be given names. What will happen to us when we have no names?'

'Of course you have names,' exclaimed Baelon, 'but they are secret, sacred names as is fitting for new-born innocents like you. Come, I'll whisper your name in your ear – and don't worry, the Rescuer will know exactly who you are and what you are called.'

With that the puppies nestled close to Baelon and he quietly whispered each one's name in each silky ear. 'Be proud of your names,' he said, 'because they reflect exactly what you are.'

But the youngest puppy still looked unhappy. 'Baelon,' he snuffled, 'will we ever see our Mummy again? We weren't with her for very long, but we loved her so much and when I'm sad, I can still hear her crying out for us.'

'Trust me,' Baelon smiled, 'you will see her again, but you must be patient a little longer.'

It was not so long after they has spoken with Baelon that he called the puppies and told them to meet him in the fields when the dew was still on the grass. As they waited, they saw him in the distance walking slowly with a small, tired Retriever who was limping a little. She looked familiar and the youngest puppy suddenly said, 'Is that who I think it is? It is, it is! It's our Mummy! She's here!' Barking for joy, they rushed to meet her and, exhausted though she was, she enfolded them all in her paws, tears of happiness running down her face. 'I told you that she would come,' said Baelon, 'but you must let her rest now because she is very tired. She never forgot you and she has been waiting and yearning for so long to be with you again.'

And so time passed and Marcus, Laurie, Decca and the

puppies and their mother lived secure in the knowledge that one day they too would be taken over the Bridge by someone who loved them.

And the puppies' secret names? They were Faith, Hope and Charity. And their mother? She was Love.

*

The Rescuer's Tale

A short story by Caroline Byrne

It was a calm, sunny day at Rainbow Bridge & the Goldens had spent the morning doing their favourite things. Olly & his Pupstars had been running in the Fields of Gold, showing a couple of new arrivals how all their aches and pains had disappeared, healed by the magic of the Bridge.

Sonny, Rory, Paddy, JJ and the two Murphy's had been sitting on their favourite hill, shooting the breeze & watching the youngsters at play, before joining some of the others at the lake for a cooling swim. Now, replete and drowsy, after a lunch of their favourite shoshages, they were all relaxing on top of the hill in front of the cottages & discussing whether or not they could get the Pixies to play Hide and Seek the Treat.

Suddenly, Marcus stiffened and pricked up his ears. 'Someone's coming through the arch!' he exclaimed. 'And…and…they're extra special, I just know it!'

All the dogs sat up, straining their eyes towards the arch at the foot of the hill, but they could see nothing. Marcus shook his head. 'There is definitely someone coming, I just know it,' he insisted.

All the other dogs smiled at each other and resumed their prone positions, but Marcus stayed upright. He was waiting. He knew he had to wait, but he didn't know what for. It was just a few minutes later when Baelon appeared striding towards the arch. And then, suddenly, Daetia stepped through the arch and beside her was a human. Now, the dogs had seen humans at Rainbow Bridge before. When their time had come, they made the journey to collect their beloved pets and together they would cross the Bridge itself, never to be parted again.

But this human seemed different. She walked with purpose and from her exuded a great wave of love and kindness. She was chatting easily with Daetia and, as

Baelon approached them, they hugged each other.

'Who *is* that?' the dogs speculated amongst themselves. Not one of them recognised her and yet they all felt as though they knew her, somehow.

Daetia made her farewell & the human briefly rested her hand on the Unicorn's mane and they bowed to each other. Then she and Baelon made their way towards the waiting dogs.

'Everyone,' said Baelon, 'this is Charis. Now, of course, every human that arrives at Rainbow Bridge is special, but Charis is extra special.'

'Extra specially special?' asked Olly, apparently the only dog not struck dumb by this unusual visit.

Normally, when a human arrived, their dogs recognised them instantly and all was excitement and joy, and to be honest, (because this is Golden Retrievers we're talking about, I'm sure the other breeds are a little more circumspect), a bit chaotic. This was different. Not one of the dogs had met Charis before and yet they all felt as though they knew her.

'Yes, little Olly, extra specially special,' smiled Baelon. 'She's a Rescuer. Rescuers devote their lives to helping dogs who have no one to care for them. They do their very best to make sure that every dog that needs their help is placed in a loving forever home. Rescuers often work together to make sure they can help as many dogs as possible.'

Some of the dogs exchanged glances and then Paddy spoke for them all. 'I know that many of us here didn't have the best start in life. We were unwanted by our original owners and were either turned out to fend for ourselves or sent to the Pound. Or even,' he lowered his voice, 'killed ... It's because of people like you, Charis, that the lucky ones, like me, were rehomed and knew love and kindness and safety.'

'And treats!' cried Leah and they all laughed, as the tension was broken.

Charis smiled at the gathered dogs. 'I am proud to have been able to help so many of you. The stories my friends and I heard from the families lucky enough to have been matched with one of our rescues made our hearts sing with joy and we were all determined to keep helping dogs who needed us for as long as we possibly could.'

Baelon then spoke. 'Charis now has a very special final task to do. As a Rescuer, she is entitled to take any dogs who didn't have a family of their own across the Bridge. Step forward please Decca, Marcus, Laurie, Faith, Hope, Charity and Love.'

The seven dogs looked at each other in delight. They had thought that they were destined to stay for a very long time at Rainbow Bridge. They had accepted that Rescuers came along all too rarely and they had watched with a strange kind of longing as other dogs had been reunited with their humans and crossed the Bridge together.

Now this person had appeared and suddenly it seemed their journey was not yet finished, after all. Marcus stepped forward, followed by the others, the puppies, Faith Hope and Charity tripping and bouncing in their excitement. Charis knelt and held out her arms to them all and they were all enveloped in her love.

'Now, say your farewells,' said Baelon, 'your time has come.'

The other dogs exchanged happy glances, they knew what to do and they loved this ritual. Charis got to her feet, Hope, the smallest puppy still in her arms. As she and Baelon turned towards the Bridge they were greeted by the sight of a Golden guard of honour, lining their path. As the little band passed each pair, the dogs bowed low. Finally, they reached the great stone steps and Charis bade Baelon farewell.

She and her dogs started to climb the steps while the sound of joyful barking from the gathered Goldens floated up to them. At the top of the steps, Charis turned for the final time and raised her hand, sending one last wave of love washing over the Golden pack.

Then she turned and together with her band crossed the Bridge, heading over the rainbow to everlasting happiness.

*

Kevin

A Short Story by Ian O'Neill

Baelon sat alone and thoughtful on the hill staring into space. Guardian of Rainbow Bridge was a job he loved, and though demanding, he thrived on the responsibility of the dogs' welfare being his. Together with his Elven and Pixie friends, they could make their stay at Rainbow Bridge as happy as possible. The dogs would miss their families terribly, but the beautiful surroundings and abundance of love would go a long way to healing their hurt.

But it was the lost and abandoned dogs that broke his heart. Many would have suffered ill health before they passed, some even cruelty. The magic of Rainbow Bridge offered an instant cure to any physical illnesses and injuries, but the emotional traumas took longer. Their healing was a potent combination of Elven holistic medicine and love from the dogs. The camaraderie between them was something that never failed to gladden his heart. Was he the luckiest Elf alive to see such a thing? He thought so.

Daetia appeared through the arch at the foot of the hill with their latest guest. He always waited and let her talk to the dogs, to reassure them and prepare them for the next stage of their journey. The Unicorn exuded love and kindness and even the most traumatised of dogs responded to her special gift. He waited for her signal and then climbed to his feet and slowly walked towards them.

His worst fears were confirmed as he approached them. This poor dog looked emaciated and beaten, not in a physical sense but his life, as short as it had been, had worn him down. Careful and skilful handling was going to be required.

He took a deep breath and composed himself and said as cheerily as he could, 'Daetia, who do we have here?'

Her sad eyes told him all he needed to know. The dog looked drained of energy and emotion. Daetia looked on the verge of tears.

'This is Kevin, Baelon. He has been extremely ill.'

Baelon crouched down and stroked the fur around Kevin's neck. Kevin didn't speak or even acknowledge the Elf's presence. He stood there looking lost and bewildered.

'Welcome to Rainbow Bridge, my young friend. I am the Guardian of the Bridge and will make sure you are well looked after.'

'He's very weak,' said Daetia. 'He will need extra special care.'

'And he will get it, Daetia.' With that Baelon scooped up Kevin's frail body into his arms.

Daetia kissed Kevin gently on his head. 'Take care, little one, and let Rainbow Bridge heal you with its magic.'

Baelon set off up the hill with the trembling Kevin in his arms. His heart ached at the poor boy's frail condition. He tenderly whispered, 'You're safe now, little one, there's no need to be frightened.'

He strode purposefully over the brow of the hill and towards the valley below where the cottages sheltered under the shadow of the bridge, but poor Kevin was barely aware of his surroundings. Baelon couldn't wait to get him to the care of the Healers. Together with the dogs they would repair this boy, of that he was sure.

As Baelon neared the cottages he was approached by several Goldens: Maisie, Bonnie, Zara, Podge, Ziggy, Ava, Megan and Chip trotted up to him.

'Oh Baelon, what's happened to this poor dog?' asked Maisie.

He knelt down so that Kevin could see them all. 'Kevin was very ill in the human world and sadly lost the fight,' said Baelon. 'It is now up to us all to rehabilitate him, but first I will take him to the Healers. They need to build him back up.'

'Let us look after him,' pleaded Ava. 'We can care for him'.

The other Goldies nodded as one and said, 'Please Baelon.'

The Elf wasn't so sure. 'As much as I admire your noble intentions, Kevin is very weak and very frightened. He didn't have a Mummy and Daddy in the human world and was being looked after by a Rescuer. We need to build him up, not just physically, but spiritually, with food and love.'

'But we can do that,' insisted Bonnie.

Just at that moment Sonny, Rory, Max, Toby, Olly and Harvey joined them. They'd seen the others surrounding Baelon.

'What is it? What's wrong?' asked Olly.

The others stepped aside, and Olly saw the sick dog in Baelon's arms.

'Young Kevin here has been very ill,' said Maisie. 'And he doesn't have a Mummy and Daddy.'

Olly was horrified. 'Doesn't have a Mummy and Daddy?'

Harvey stepped forward and carefully sniffed Kevin. 'He's very frightened and very weak, Baelon. All of us here have been loved so much by our Mummies and Daddies. Let us share some with this young fella. We have plenty.'

Before Baelon could answer, Sonny stepped in. 'Would you like something to eat, Kevin. Some chicken maybe, or some rice?'

Kevin lay in Baelon's arms not even acknowledging the question.

'I know,' said Podge and went bounding off towards the cottages.

'I really think he needs to be in the care of the Healers. You can all come and see him once he's feeling stronger,' said Baelon sympathetically.

'But he'll feel better surrounded by us,' said Megan.

Podge came bounding back towards them with a silver dog's bowl in his mouth. He lay the bowl at Baelon's feet, and said, 'Shoshages, I've yet to find a dog who doesn't love a shoshage.'

'Genius!' said Harvey.

'Good call, Podge,' said Chip.

Baelon looked at the anticipation in all of their faces and

realised he wasn't going to take Kevin anywhere until he tried the shoshages. He gently put Kevin back on the ground and pointed towards the bowl. Kevin was so weak he just sat down and looked up at the Elf with doleful eyes.

'Feed him the shoshage by hand,' said Olly, his tail wagging furiously.

'Definitely taste better when fed by hand,' agreed Podge.

Baelon took a shoshage in his hand and held it up to Kevin's mouth. Kevin sniffed it for moment before taking it into his mouth and slowly chewing it and swallowing.

'And another,' said Olly excitedly.

Kevin took the next one and this one was eaten much quicker, followed by another and then another. By the time he got to the last one he was eating with the usual gusto of a Retriever, i.e. one bite and swallow. He stood and there was a slight hint of his tail wagging for the first time since he'd arrived at the Bridge. He looked at them all and tried to smile, but he was still very weak.

In a very shallow voice, he said, 'Wuvley'.

Harvey was beside himself with joy. 'That's what my Mummy used to say when she was writing letters from me!'

'You see, Baelon,' said Maisie, 'Kevin will heal faster with us around him.'

The Elf knew that it was an argument he couldn't win. He reminded himself that it was the dogs that did the healing, and he had to agree that Kevin's suffering wasn't just of the body but of the mind and spirit as well.

'Very well, Kevin will go with you, but on one condition. That the Healers can call on him regularly to make sure he's progressing as he should.'

'We agree,' said Sonny on behalf of them all. The Goldie pack surrounded their new friend and very carefully escorted him to the cottages. Podge walked next to Kevin making sure he didn't stumble. He whispered into his ear, 'You can share my bed, there's plenty of room. Did I tell you my Daddy's name is Kevin?'

*

Four weeks later ...

'Lionpaws!'

Furry heads appeared randomly over the top of the barley; it was like a Retriever merry- go-round. Joyful barking and laughing filled the air. It was a Golden Retriever play day, and the pack was chasing Harvey through the barley and he kept hiding which made them bark and laugh even louder.

Then after half-an-hour of frolics and fun, Harvey suddenly appeared from the barley and flopped down on the grass, exhausted. The pack followed: Sonny, Rory, Maisie, Zara, Bob, Rolo, Podge, Jake, Murphy, Harry, Alfie, Ziggy, Chip, Bonnie, Charlie H, Rooney, Charlie S, Bilbo, Honey, Sailor, Maisie H, Annie, Meggie, Molly, Charlie K, Rio W, Charlie H, Rio H, Ava, Willow, Roxy, Hannah, Oscar, Megan, Rusty, Champ and Misty.

The last one to emerge was a young Goldie. His coat was shiny and thick. His fan tail was wagging furiously. He held his head high and proud; his eyes were sharp and clear, and he bounded out onto the grass and pounced on Harvey as he lay resting. The curly one gasped at the impact but wrapped his giant paws around the youngster and licked his face.

'I love you, Lionpaws!'

'And I love you, little Kevin!'

*

Roxy's Story

A Short Story by Jennifer Small

Roxy was scared. The last thing that she remembered was lying with her head in her Mummy's lap, being gently stroked and told what a good girl she was, as she drifted off to sleep. And now she was standing in the middle of a green, sunlit field that didn't look like anywhere she knew. In front of her was a great golden arch but she was too nervous to go through it.

'Hello! There you are!' said a voice from behind her. 'I've been waiting for you to come.'

Roxy turned round to see a large white horse with a horn that seemed to be growing out of its head.

'Who are you?' she quavered. 'And where am I?'

'Of course, you don't recognise me,' said the Unicorn – for that is what it was – 'but I'm Daetia and I've come to help you to the Rainbow Bridge.'

'I don't want to go to any bridge' wailed Roxy, 'I want to go home, and I want my Mummy!'

Daetia smiled sympathetically. 'Don't you remember falling asleep in your Mummy's lap as she rubbed your ears and whispered, 'Goodbye' to you? She knew that it was time for you to go and start the next stage of your journey and this is where it all begins. Come with me, we'll walk through the arch together and meet my good friend, Baelon. He's an Elf and he'll take you to meet your sisters and your brother. Did you know that you had sisters and a brother here waiting for you? There's Morgan and Kelly, Purdey and Hannah and they've been watching for you for so long.'

'Won't my Mummy wonder where I am?' said Roxy. Daetia smiled gently and replied, 'She's knows exactly where you are and though she misses you dreadfully, she is sure that this is where you are supposed to be now. Look, here's Baelon – he'll take you now.'

'Hello, my little one,' Baelon greeted Roxy, 'Let's go

the rest of the way together.' So off they set across that sunny field under a great glowing rainbow that curved protectively above them. Some way in the distance, where the rainbow seemed to end, Roxy could just see a flower-strewn bridge. 'Is that where we are going?' she asked Baelon. 'No,' he said, 'not yet, that's for a time to come.'

'It's just a few steps more,' he encouraged her as Roxy started to trail behind, 'we're nearly there and I can see Morgan, Purdey, Kelly and Hannah waiting for you.'

'How do I know who's who?' asked Roxy nervously. 'Well,' said Baelon, 'Kelly is Purdey's Mum and Hannah is the one with the crinkle on her nose. Come and meet them.'

But Roxy lingered reluctant to go any further. 'What's wrong, little one?' asked Baelon.

'I'm afraid that they won't like me,' whispered Roxy. 'They'll laugh at me'.

'Why should they do that?' asked Baelon, surprised.

Roxy looked shamefaced and said, 'I've only got half a tail – someone chopped half of it off when I was little and now I look odd.'

Baelon laughed. 'I think you'll find that there's nothing wrong with your tail – look at it!'

So Roxy looked over her shoulder and there was the most magnificent, flowing tail you could ever imagine! 'My tail's back!' she exclaimed in delight, 'how did that happen?'

'Well, when you come to the Rainbow Bridge', Baelon explained, 'all the things that were wrong with you or were hurting you are immediately cured – so you have your tail back again!'

With that, Roxy felt confident enough to put her trust in Baelon and go with him to meet her brother and sisters. They ran up to her, and Hannah, whose nose was even more crinkled up with joy, nuzzled and licked her in welcome. 'We've been watching out for you, little sister,' they woofed, 'because we wanted to make sure that we were the first to welcome you home! Do you remember what Mummy used to call our 'exhibition runs' when we ran around and around in huge circles? Let's do one now!'.

But Roxy looked rather unsure. 'I don't think that I can,' she apologised. 'I had an operation on my leg and I'm a bit old and wobbly on my paws now.'

'Yes, you can', the others chorused. 'We're all like young pups again here – no more aches and pains and we can run forever.' True to their word, off they went calling Roxy to follow. 'Come on,' encouraged Hannah, 'you can do it!'

And so she could. She ran and ran like the wind catching her sisters and brother in great joyous circles, her newly restored tail streaming out behind her until they flopped down panting to drink from a clear crystal stream.

Hannah noticed that Roxy had become very withdrawn again. 'What's wrong, my sister?' she asked quietly. 'What's going to happen to me now?' asked Roxy nervously. 'Who will look after me? Where am I going to live?' Hannah smiled. 'You'll live with us in our cottage, of course. The Elves look after us; they've already made you a lovely soft bed and there's a dinner bowl just for you with your name on it.'

'Did you say 'dinner'? I think that it's time for our dinner now,' said Kelly jumping to her feet. 'We have all sorts of lovely food and our bowls are always full; in fact, anything that you want just simply appears by magic! Come on, little sister!'

But Roxy still lagged behind suddenly overcome by a wave of sorrow. 'Won't I ever see my Mummy again? I miss her so much,' she sniffed, a large tear trickling down her snout.

'Of course you will,' Hannah replied, comforting her with a gentle paw. 'When it's her time, she'll come through the arch and under the rainbow too and she'll find us again and we'll all cross the Bridge together; until then you are wrapped up safe in her heart as we all are, and because she loves us so, she'll never forget us. If we think about her hard enough, we can go to her in her dreams and while she's sleeping she'll know that we are lying beside her bed watching over her like we always used to do.'

So Roxy, content in the knowledge that she would see her loved ones again, joined her sisters and brother in the land under the Rainbow. And there she lives to this day, bright-eyed and light-hearted, until the time comes at last to cross the Bridge.

*

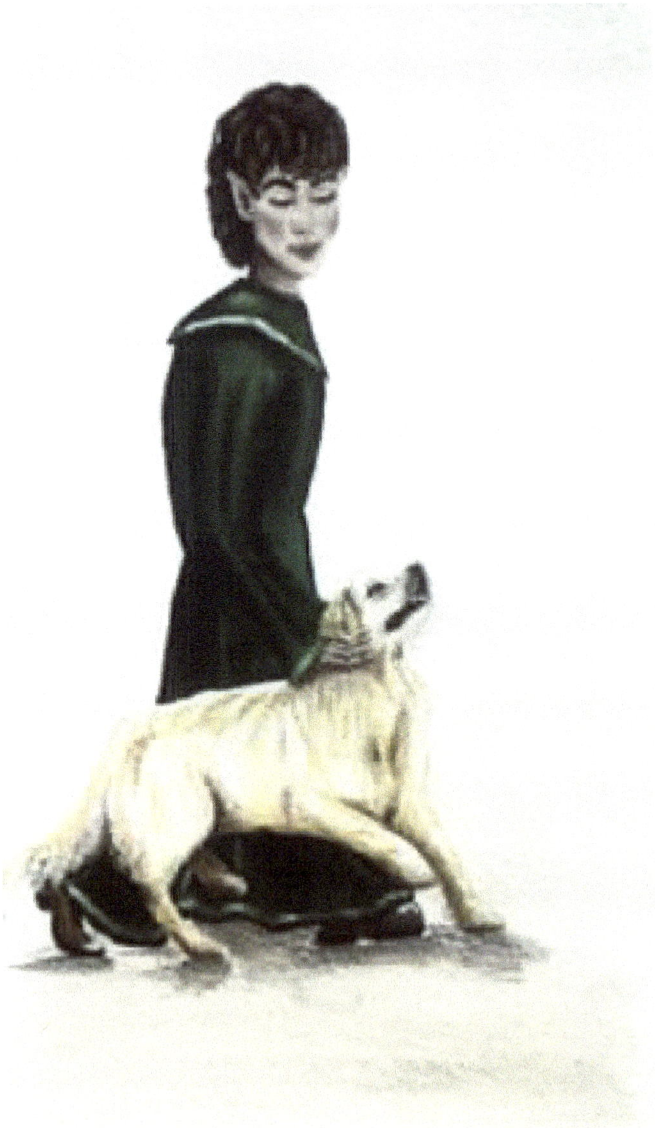

Paddy and Murphy

A Short Story by Ian O'Neill

Murphy ran through the lush, rolling meadow and into the wood. He splashed in the stream and came charging out to roll on the grass. He lay on his back looking up at the trees. Sunrays broke through the branches bathing him in their soothing warmth. He loved to be on his own. He loved being with the Goldie pack too, but he needed that time on his own. When Sonny once asked him why, he replied, 'I need my thinking time and I can't do it when other dogs are around me.'

And they accepted that Murphy needed his own space and time.

Murphy had always been a loner, even in the hooman world. He could take or leave either dogs or people. Except his Mummy. Murphy loved his Mummy with every ounce of his being. She was the only one who understood him. She understood his need to be left on his own. His life on Rainbow Bridge had changed markedly after his mother came to see him one night. Just being with her made everything right. He would see her again of that he was sure.

Today, he had his breakfast early and then relaxed for an hour with his friends. When Olly and the Pupstars ran off to the Fields of Gold, Murphy took his opportunity and quietly slipped off through the meadow and beyond. He ran. Then ran some more. Running was freedom to Murphy. The first thing all the older dogs who arrived at Rainbow Bridge noticed was that their limbs and body were pain free. Arthritis didn't exist on the Bridge. Even if their bodies had been ravaged by cancer, their youthful vitality would return.

And they would always want to run. Usually with Olly through the Fields of Gold.

Murphy spent the day running from one place to another with the occasional rest and a drink from a freshwater stream. Rainbow Bridge always seemed new and fresh. No two days were ever the same. Baelon the Elf said that was due to the magic. But it didn't matter to Murphy, as long as there was fresh air, fields, woods, streams and hills to run up and down, he was content.

As afternoon inevitably drifted through to evening Murphy climbed a rolling hill and sat at the top and marvelled at the beauty of his surroundings. He looked back towards the cottages in the distance and the Fields of Gold on top of the hill beyond. He looked across the fields towards the golden arch and thought of home.

He sat quietly reflecting on his day when he noticed another Golden sat on top of the next hill along. Whoever it was sat gazing across the landscape completely unaware of Murphy. It was unusual, although not unheard of, to see a Golden on their own in the hills away from the cottages. They would usually run as a pack. Murphy was about to go back to the cottages in time for his tea but saw no harm in running across and asking if the Golden wanted to run back with him.

He set off down the hill then up towards the lone Golden. He slowed down as he approached as he didn't want to startle them. He slowed to a walk and was only a few metres away. The other Golden sat trance like staring across towards the golden arch and didn't notice Murphy approaching. Murphy momentarily thought about turning around and leaving them to their thoughts when they didn't notice him, but his nose suddenly caught a familiar scent.

It reminded him of something. Something very special. The other golden turned around and Murphy immediately saw the fear in his eyes.

'I'm sorry, I didn't mean to startle you. Only it's nearly supper time and I wondered if you wanted to run back with me?'

The other Golden didn't reply. Murphy hadn't seen him before and assumed that he lived in one of the other cottages. 'I can leave you on your own if you would prefer, only …'

'I'm frightened.'

Murphy could see it. Not just in his eyes. It was his whole body language.

'I only arrived today.'

Murphy remembered how bewildered he felt when he first arrived on the Bridge.

'It's OK to be frightened. We all are when we first arrive. The Elves will help you settle in and the Goldies here are all friendly and supportive.'

'They asked if I wanted to run in the Fields of Gold, but I preferred to be on my own.'

Murphy smiled to himself. It was Olly's stock question to all new Goldies when they arrived.

'What's your name, my friend? My name is Murphy.'

'Paddy.'

'Welcome to Rainbow Bridge, Paddy.'

'I want to go home. I want to go back to my Mummy and Theo and Lexie.'

'Did you say Theo and Lexie? What's your surname?'

'I'm Paddy Byrne.'

That was it. The scent he could smell was home. His Mummy's perfume; the house; the garden. His Mummy had told him about his two younger brothers and sister when she visited.

'My name is Murphy Byrne. I'm your big brother.'

Paddy looked at Murphy wide eyed in amazement.

'You're my brother?'

Murphy nodded.

'We have the same Mummy?'

Murphy nodded again.

'I am glad you are my brother. I feel less frightened now.'

'There is no need for you to ever be frightened again, little bro. And your sister Daisy is here too and visits the cottages where we stay.'

'I liked Daisy. She was kind to me.'

'She has a sweet nature,' agreed Murphy.

'I'm not sure where I sleep, or where my new home is. I ran straight here once Baelon had introduced me.'

'You will have your own bed and sleep next to me, little bro. If there is anything you're not sure about, just ask.'

Paddy looked at Murphy, tears glistened his eyes. 'I am glad I have my brother here.'

Murphy stood up and stretched his legs. 'Come, little bro, let's head back to the cottages. Shoshages for tea tonight, with thick gravy.'

'I love shoshages,' said Paddy. 'They are my favourite. Although I had to watch Theo like a hawk just in case he tried to pinch mine.'

Paddy stood up and walked down the hill alongside his brother. 'I am upset because I heard our Mummy crying as I walked through the mist.'

Murphy looked sad. 'She would've been devastated to lose you, Paddy. She fought for all her dogs. We are so lucky that she's our Mummy.'

'I am going to miss her. I am going to miss her with all my heart,' said Paddy.

Murphy stopped and turned to his brother. 'If I tell you something will you promise to keep it a secret.'

Paddy nodded.

'Our Mummy came to see me one night.'

Paddy looked confused. 'Here? On Rainbow Bridge?'

Murphy nodded. 'I sat outside our cottages as I couldn't sleep, and she appeared out of the shadows. Oh, Paddy, I thought my heart would burst with joy. We walked around the blue lake together under the stone bridge.'

'But how did she get here?'

'She has a friend. She called him the Chronicler. He walks Rainbow Bridge and writes our stories. I think he made it possible.'

'Our Mummy named the Chronicler,' said Paddy proudly.

It was Murphy's turn to look confused. 'Named him?'

'Yes, she said he writes lovely stories about Rainbow Bridge, so she called him the Chronicler.'

'He is a mystery man. Everybody knows him, but nobody knows him,' said Murphy.

'I have no idea what that means,' said Paddy.

'Nor do I,' smiled Murphy.

They trotted silently alongside each other for a while. Paddy kept within his own thoughts and Murphy gave his brother the space to do just that. As they approached the cottages Paddy stopped.

'Would you mind if I have a few minutes on my own?'

'Of course,' said Murphy. 'I'll wait outside our cottage for you.'

As Murphy trotted off towards the cottages, Paddy slowly walked up the side of the hill. At the top he had a clear view of the golden arch. The arch that only a matter of hours ago he'd walked through with the Unicorn. He sat down and looked up into the evening sky. He breathed in the fresh air and reflected on how beautiful it looked. In fact, Rainbow Bridge was beautiful. He knew he was going to like it, especially as he'd met his brother and was happy that he would soon see his sister Daisy.

But at this precise moment he wanted his Mummy. He wanted the woman who had rescued him all those years ago when others had given up on him. She was the only hooman who understood him. They'd spent many hours together where she patiently helped him to feel loved and secure in his home. And he did. For the first time ever, he felt like he belonged and that was down to that special woman who believed in him.

He looked longingly over to the golden arch and whispered words that were only for his Mummy. Words that only she would understand. 'Thank you Mummy. Thank you for believing in me when so many in my life didn't. For understanding me when no-one else did. I was rejected before I met you and I thought you would reject me too. But you didn't. You stood by me. I know I wasn't easy to handle at first, but I learnt from you that I didn't need to be frightened anymore. You showed me I belonged. I loved being part of your family. I loved Daisy and Lexie, and I didn't even mind when you brought Theo into our house.

Though he did annoy me sometimes.

I have met my big brother, Murphy, and he is as special as you said he was. He will look after me until I find my paws. He says that you have been to see him. I want you to come to see us both when you can. I'm sure the Chronicler will help you.

I am going to miss you my darling Mummy. I am going to miss the cuddles and our walks together. I am going to miss you talking to me. I am going to miss you.'

He sat back and let the gentle breeze carry his words home to his Mummy. Before turning to join his brother he said one final thing; 'I love you, Mummy. I always will. Until we meet again.'

*

A Letter from Murph

A Short Story by Ian O'Neill

'My life, whether short or long, was an enviable one. I caressed this world with my smile, bathed it with gentleness and wrung every last drop of joy from each and every day. So when the annals of canine history are written, sing no sad songs or cry sad tears for this auld fella. For I was, I am, and I will always be, a Golden Retriever ...'

Hello Mam and Dad,

Well, I arrived safely on Rainbow Bridge. It was just as you said it would be Dad. I walked through the mist and followed the voice. And I wasn't frightened because I knew you were both with me in spirit.

Then I saw her. The most beautiful Unicorn standing in front of the golden arch. Her coat was as white and pure as freshly settled snow on a crisp winter's day. She smiled warmly and beckoned me to her. I slowly walked up to her and she lowered her head and placed a kiss on me nose. I felt her tears wash over me and all the pain and illness fell away. I felt like a young dog again.

She gazed lovingly down at me and said, 'Welcome, Murphy. My name is Daetia, and I will take you through the arch. The next stage of your life journey has begun. You will soon be safely within the loving care of the Elves on Rainbow Bridge.'

We walked through the arch together and stopped on the other side. I was looking across a lush, green meadow covered in multi-coloured wildflowers. A cool and gentle breeze carried their inviting scent and made me nose twitch in appreciation. A tremendous feeling of peace and tranquillity settled over me.

I had arrived on Rainbow Bridge.

Daetia told me not to be afraid and that someone would be escorting me to the Bridge. Then she lifted her head and looked out across the meadow. I followed her gaze and saw somebody walking down the hill towards me. I knew it was an Elf because you told me, Dad. But it wasn't Baelon. A beautiful young Aelf, (female Elf), walked up to me and knelt down. She wrapped her arms around me and tenderly kissed me on the head, and said, 'Welcome to Rainbow Bridge, Murphy. My name is Aletha. I am to be your guide.'

Well, Mam and Dad, she had a presence like no other. I felt secure and loved. It was like being back with you all. I was ready to go with her.

'Murphy, I will leave you with Aletha,' said Daetia. 'She will take you to your new home on Rainbow Bridge. I want you to remember that my love is always there for you as is the love of your family. Run free, special boy.' She leant down and snuggled me once again.

Aletha stood and said, 'Come, Murphy, there are many waiting to meet you.'

She walked slowly up the hill and I trotted by her side. I couldn't help wondering why anyone would be waiting to meet me. I'm just Murphy O'Neill the cheeky little Irish dog. Well, as we approached the brow of the hill I saw two dogs trotting towards us. They stopped just a few yards in front of me and I immediately recognised one of them. I'd know that curly cream coat anywhere.

It was our Rory.

I ran to him and we had the most amazing snuggle.

The conversations went as follows: -

'Jeez, Rory, it's grand to see you,' sez I.

'You too, little bro. Here, let me introduce you to our older bro. Murph, meet Sonny-Boy,' sez he.

Well I have to admit to having a tear in me aul eye as me big bro snuggled me. I'd heard you talk about him many times and here I was having a cuddle with him. Then Rory joined us, and the three O'Neill boys had a quiet moment together. Alesha looked on and I could sense she felt the emotion that was flowing between us.

'Oh boys, that makes my heart almost burst with joy. Come let us meet your friends.'

As we reached the brow of the hill, a howl went up from

far to our left, and was responded to with another one to our right. I looked at me bros and they just smiled. We trotted forwards another few paces and I looked down the other side of the hill and it was covered with dogs and as they saw us, they all started to jump up and down and bark. I have to own up to being a bit confused.

'They're all here for you, little bro,' sez Sonny.

'Me? But why?'

'Because,' sez Rory, 'you're a legend, our Murph.'

'Me? A legend?'

'You are indeed,' sez Sonny. 'You have a rare and precious gift.'

'I think you may be getting me mixed up with someone else. I have no gifts unless you call hoovering me food up in 10 seconds flat a gift!'

'We all have that gift,' smiled Rory. 'Sonny's talking about something else.'

'You have the gift of making people smile,' sez Sonny. 'You radiate happiness wherever you go. We watched you walking up the hill towards us. Your tail was wagging, and your face was smiling.'

'I don't see the point in being miserable,' sez I. 'Our aul fella told me exactly what was happening, so I wasn't frightened.'

'But don't you feel sad at leaving home?' asked Rory.

'Of course I do,' sez I. 'But I was pretty ill back there, Rory. I knew it was me time.'

'Happy and wise, a great combination,' sez Rory.

'Let's meet the Golden gang,' sez Sonny. 'They're all dying to meet you.'

So the three brothers trotted down the hill alongside Aletha as the Rainbow Bridge welcome reached its crescendo. It appeared that the whole of Rainbow Bridge came out to welcome me. The noise was deafening. I walked proudly alongside me two brothers towards the waiting Golden Retrievers outside the cottages. As we approached them, I saw someone I recognised. It was only me aul mate Paddy B. Jeez, it was grand to see him again.

He ran over to me and gave me the biggest snuggle.

'Murphy,' sez he, 'it's so good to see you again. You're looking well.'

'I'm looking a lot better than I was a few hours ago,' sez I. 'Jeez Paddy I felt as rough as a half-chewed dog's bone!'

'That's rough,' sez he. 'Here, meet me big bro. And guess what his name is? It's only Murphy, the same as you.'

Then Murphy gave me the traditional Rainbow Bridge snuggle.

'This could get confusing,' sez I.

'You can be Murphy O, and me bro can be Murphy B,' sez Paddy.

'Grand so,' sez I.

'Come little bro,' sez Rory. 'There are introductions to be made.'

The barking stopped and it felt like all eyes were on me. A succession of Goldens stepped forward and were introduced. For the life of me, I can't remember all their names. But then I saw two that I knew. A beautiful girl walked up to me and dropped a tennis ball at me feet.

'Hello Murphy. Do you remember me?'

'Of course I do,' sez I. 'It's grand to see you again, Lottie. You're looking well.'

'We can play with my ball when you've settled. The Pixies will throw the ball all day for us.'

'Sounds like doggie heaven,' sez I.

'That's exactly what it as,' laughed Paddy and the others.

Then guess who came up to me? Still a giant and the same aul gentle smile. It was only Jackson. We had a fine aul snuggle. As you can probably imagine, me aul head was spinning by this time.

Another couple of oldies came up to and give me a snuggle. Their names were Brody and Monty. And then Monty's sister, Totty, gave me a snuggle. They were all so kind to me.

Then Sonny introduced me to another Goldie. He called her the Mammy of them all. Her name was Maisie. Well, she knew how to snuggle right enough. Made me go a little weak at the knees. And you'll never guess who her Mammy is back in the hooman world? Only me Auntie Lesley. I told her that her Mammy was in good form and still gives the best cuddles. Our Maisie got a little tearful, so it was my turn to snuggle her.

And then this young fella comes bounding up to me like a whirlwind. 'Murphy,' sez he. 'You're a legend!'

'So I believe,' sez I.

'Do you want to run with me in the Fields of Gold?' sez he, now jumping up and down and his tail wagging frantically.

'Meet Olly,' smiled Sonny. 'All new arrivals get to run through the Fields.'

'Sounds like great fun,' sez I.

'So let's do it,' sez Rory.

A pack of Goldens ran as one up the hill to the rear of the cottages and disappeared into the tall golden barley. Well, I can't remember the last time I ran so fast and for so long. I had a grand aul time.

*

That was over two weeks ago. I'm now sitting in front of the Fields of Gold looking out across the blue lake towards the golden arch on the far side of the Bridge. Me thoughts are with you at home and me aul heart aches for you all. It's all been a bit frantic since I arrived. I've been playing every day and meeting new friends. It's been grand enough but exhausting too.

It was Sonny that took me to one side and said maybe I needed some time to meself. He said that many of the dogs come up here to be alone. It's the place where they send their messages back home.

So here I am.

So many things to say. Where do I start? I want to thank you both for saving me. Me life back in Ireland wasn't looking great. Me aul prospects were bleak. Well, at least they were until the lady from IRR came for me. I spent some time with her in Ireland before I was put in a crate and travelled across the sea to England. I was taken to a lovely lady called Amy, and she was me foster carer. I spent a few weeks with her, and I had a great mate in her dog, Nugget, although if I'm honest, I gave the poor fecker a hell of a time. But me excuse was that I was young.

And then I got brought over to meet you both. You took me out for a walk, and I met me brother, Rory. Now he wasn't that keen on me at first with good reason, as I plagued the life out of the poor aul fella. But we got used to each other and I got to learn when Rory wanted to rest and when he wanted to play.

But what made me realise that you were me forever, Mammy and Daddy, was when Duke the Dane attacked me just a few days after arriving at me new home. Dad, you somehow managed to fight him off and get me back home unscathed. And when I saw the state of your hand with all the blood, I knew I was going to be looked after for the rest of me natural days.

I was well and truly home.

What followed were many happy times spent together as a family. First, with Rory and then with Luce. Jeez, she gave me a run for me money when she first arrived. I was on the receiving end of some of what I'd dished out to Rory. But we became great friends and had many a grand run together.

We moved down to Somerset three years ago. Well, me and Luce thought all our Christmases had come at once. We got to run on beaches every week. It was pawsome, (that's an Olly word by the way).

And then the big fella joined us. Or as you called him, the gentle giant. And he was. Henry seemed to know that I wasn't up to full on bitey face although we did have a gentle play sometimes. They were happy days indeed.

I've had a great life with your all. I well and truly fell on me paws when I came to you. And I want you to know that you both did the right thing by me the other week. I was ready to go and gave you the look. I was with the two people I loved most in the world. You held me and whispered words that will forever remain a secret. I felt both of your tears falling on me as I drifted off into me final sleep.

I want you to know that Rainbow Bridge is a magical place. There is no illness, and all the dogs are looked after. We want for nothing. I've had shoshages for me tea every evening. There's an auld fella called Podge who is known as the shoshage monster. He's a grand aul chap.

Young Olly keeps us all amused with his chasing games and endless energy. He has a group of youngsters who follow him, and they're called the Pupstars. They are a grand bunch of pups who keep us all on our toes.

Me, Sonny, Rory, Paddy B, Murphy B, Max, Toby, Brody, Monty, Jackson and Jake are known as the 'Likely Lads'. We spend hours running through the green meadows and up and down the rolling hills. We're all amazed at just how much energy we have now, but that's down to the magic of the Bridge.

I'm hoping that this letter finds its way to you both. I'm told that there is a mystery fella called the Chronicler who writes about us all on the Bridge. They say everybody knows him, but nobody knows him. Whatever the feck that means!

Can you make sure you tell all your pals that us dogs on the Bridge are fine and happy? Well as happy as we can be without our families. I've been home to see you all. I come in the night when you're all asleep. I sit and watch your and it fills me aul heart with joy. I sometimes share a bed with Luce or Henry. They know I'm there, it's like I never left you all.

I'm not going to lie, if I had the choice I would've stayed with you all forever. I would never want to leave. Me dream would be for us all to walk across the Rainbow Bridge together as a family. But that's not possible at this time. Life is what it is, and we take whatever hand we get dealt.

But I'm happy. I'm happy that I got to spend all those years with you. That we shared the experiences we did, both good and bad. And I wait here with me brothers and we talk about home. All of us lay outside the cottages of a night and we reminisce. Sure, there are a few tears, but there is lots of laughter too.

I plan to write regularly so you know what's going on up here. I have many stories to tell. I just want you to know that I love you both with all me heart. Give Luce and Henry a big hug and kiss from their elder brother.

For now, your happy and smiling auld fella, Murph.

*

Martha and Darcy

A Short Story by Ian O'Neill

'Come on Darcy, no excuses. We're going for a run together.'

Martha stood on the veranda of the cottage looking disapprovingly down at her brother as he lay on the grass.

'But I'm going out with the Likely Lads,' pleaded Darcy.

'You go out with the Likely Lads every day. It's time you went out with your sister.'

Murphy O, Teal, Paddy B and Murphy B looked on in silence, not daring to confront the formidable Martha.

'But I've promised,' said Darcy.

Darcy looked up at his sister and saw an expression on her face that he'd seen many times before. He knew she wasn't going to give in. If there was one word you could use to describe Martha, it was stubborn. Darcy reluctantly dragged himself to his feet and did a full body stretch. He turned to his pals. 'It looks like I'm going out with Martha today.'

The four friends nodded that they understood, and Murphy O whispered under his breath, 'Jeez, and I thought our Luce was bossy.'

Martha turned her steely gaze towards him. 'Something to say, Murphy?'

'Er, just wishing you both a grand day out.' He turned to his pals. 'Come on lads, let's get out of here.' And the four of them sped off across the meadow.

Martha turned her attention back to Darcy. 'Right, let's go.'

Darcy sighed in resignation and trotted by his sister's side as they headed out across the meadow. As they climbed the hill Martha broke into a run and Darcy ran by her side. She turned to him and said, 'Where will the Likely Lads go first?'

'Straight to the wood to play in the pond,' said Darcy.

'We'll go to Rainbow Hill and sit on the top. There are views all across the Bridge from there.'

Darcy nodded and the two of them headed towards the hill in the distance. Once they reached the top Martha sat down and caught her breath. Darcy sat down by her side and followed her gaze across the beautiful landscape. It was a place he'd often visit with his pals, and he never tired of the spectacular views. He gazed a cross to the wood where the Likely Lads would by now be splashing around like mad things in the green slimy pond.

He wondered why his sister suddenly decided she wanted to spend the day with him when she would normally be with her pals Shannon, Maisie and Zara doing whatever it was they do. He also knew there was no point in pushing her for answers as she would tell him when she was good and ready.

Martha continued to gaze out across the green fields. Darcy fidgeted restlessly next to her. After several minutes she turned to him. 'Has Olly ever told you about the dreams he has, the ones where he's back at home with his family?'

Darcy nodded. 'Many times. I quite envy him. I never dream, well other than when I'm chasing rabbits, but we all have those.'

'Do you ever think of home?' asked Martha.

'Every day,' said Darcy.

'They were good times, weren't they?'

'The best,' said Darcy. 'Except of course when you conned me out of my bones.'

Martha smiled at the memory. 'And you fell for it every time.'

'You were too quick for me, Martha. You still are.'

'I look out for you though, don't I, Darcy.'

'You do. You're not a bad sister, even though you nag me all the time.'

'I'm just keeping you out of mischief,' smiled Martha.

'So, why the questions about home?' asked Darcy.

'I had that dream last night,' said Martha.

'What dream?' asked Darcy.

'Olly's dream where I was back home. Only it didn't feel like a dream, it felt real.'

'Did you see our Mam?'

An expression of happiness coupled with sadness crossed her face. 'I sat by her bed and watched her as she slept. Oh Darcy, I can't begin to describe the feelings I had.'

Darcy was silent for a moment. He first gazed out across the fields and then back at his sister. 'How do you have this dream?'

'I wish I knew, Darcy, it just happened. I pray I have it again.'

'Can you pray for me having it too?' he asked hopefully.

She reached across and placed her paw on top of his. 'Of course I will my lovely brother.'

*

Darcy walked carefully and silently along the floor making sure it didn't creak. He sat watching her for several moments as she slept. He lay his head on the pillow next to her and breathed, 'I miss you, Mam. Martha misses you too. We're waiting, we're always waiting …'

*

A Golden Fellowship

A Short Story by Ian O'Neill

Two young Goldens sprung from the tall barley and slumped onto the lush green grass. They lay on their bellies, pink tongues hanging from their mouths, breathing heavily following their exertions.

'That was brilliant,' gasped Olly in between breaths.

'It was indeed!' agreed Buddy. 'Where's Zoe and Kevin?'

'Still looking for me,' smiled Olly. 'You're the only one who's caught me all week.'

Olly rolled over onto his back and wriggled like an electric eel. He groaned as if he was in ecstasy. 'Ooh that's lovely. Can you give my back a scratch, Buddy? I think I have bits of barley seed in my coat.'

Buddy reached across and scratched Olly's back with his front right paw.

'Up a bit, down a bit, just by the right shoulder. That's it, ooh that's pawfect.'

Buddy started to chuckle. 'I love it when you make up words.'

'That's a proper Goldie word,' said Olly proudly. 'Describes pawfectly what I'm trying to say,' he laughed, as Buddy carried on scratching his shoulder. 'Buddy, you are just the best back scratcher.'

'Lionpaws says the same,' said Buddy. 'He said that my back scratches are awesome.'

'Don't you mean pawsome?' smiled Olly. 'And Lionpaws would know as that curly coat takes some scratching!'

They both lay down on their bellies and adopted the 'sphinx' pose and stared out across the Bridge. A mild sun rested over the hills, casting a warm, healing glow across the beautiful landscape. Rainbow Bridge was always picturesque, but the warm sunshine made it even more so.

'I never tire of looking across the lake towards the arch,' said Olly.

'Me neither,' said Buddy. 'I often hope that …'

Olly looked over to his friend and could sense his sadness. 'It's OK, Buddy. We all look at that arch in hope at times.'

Buddy didn't answer for a few moments. He seemed lost in his thoughts. 'I've been thinking about home a lot lately.'

Olly didn't comment and let his friend carry on.

'I was young like you when I left home. Daetia told me that I had been really ill and that the Healers couldn't help me. Sometimes I miss my Mummy and Daddy terribly.'

Olly reached across and rested his right paw on top of Buddy's front paws. 'It was the same for me. I remember little of what happened just before I arrived here.'

'Me neither,' said Buddy. 'Maybe it's for the best?'

Olly turned towards his friend and nodded. 'I think so.'

'I loved my home, Olly. My Mummy and Daddy were so kind to me. I spent every waking moment with them. I used to lay on my Daddy as he sat in his chair and he would stroke me. And sometimes I would fall asleep and feel his soft breath on my head. I felt so loved, Olly, and so safe. And the walks in the countryside and the woods were brilliant. I would run and run and find amazing smells everywhere and chase squirrels. I thought my heart would burst with happiness.'

He looked across to Olly, tears glistening his eyes. 'And then it all went, just disappeared into nothing.'

'We all miss home,' said Olly, 'but sometimes we need to remind ourselves of the great bond there is between us all here. We all love you, Buddy. You're the kindest of the kind. In fact, you're one of my best buddies.'

Buddy looked at Olly and raised his eyes. A trace of a smile crossed his lips. 'You never fail to cheer me up, Olly, but your jokes leave a lot to be desired.'

'Ha-ha, that's what Max and Toby say.'

'Thanks Olly, you're a good friend to me. As are Zoe and Kevin.'

'Everyone on Rainbow Bridge is your friend, Buddy. And if you're feeling down, go to see Maisie, she gives the best snuggles and she always has some soothing words to make you feel better. Or talk to Lionpaws, he is just so wise, or Podge, Sonny, Rory, Chip, Ziggy, Paddy, Murphy. They all love you Buddy, and all understand your pain.'

Buddy rubbed his eyes with his paw. Olly's words had really helped him - but they always did. 'How does someone so young get to be so wise?'

Olly smiled. 'I don't think Max and Toby would agree; they're always telling me to slow down and take it easy. But I can't, I have to squeeze every last drop of enjoyment from each and every day.' He sat quietly for a moment and cast his gaze over towards the golden arch. 'I've learnt that if I think about home before I go to sleep, then my dreams take me back there. I see Bennie, Bailey, and I see my Mummy asleep. I lay my head on her pillow and just watch her. Oh Buddy, I can't begin to explain the feelings of love that run through my body.'

Just at that moment two Goldens came charging out of the tall barley.

'So here you are!' squealed Zoe. 'Kevin and I have been searching everywhere.'

Kevin threw himself on top of Olly and the two pals rolled around on the lush grass playing bitey face. Zoe joined in and Buddy jumped up and ran around them barking with glee. It was a Golden bundle, a scene which many of us have witnessed numerous times. It quite possibly could have gone on for hours, but their fun was interrupted by the faint sound of a gong in the distance.

Kevin jumped up and stood looking down the hill towards the cottages. 'It's tea-time! And it's shoshages tonight. Quick everyone, let's get back before Podge eats them all!'

And with that they all jumped up and ran as fast as their legs would carry them down the hill. Olly turned to Buddy as they ran side by side and mouthed the word, *'dreams'* to him. Buddy nodded that he understood.

*

Buddy crept quietly over the bedroom floor and stopped and watched his Daddy as he peacefully slept. He thought his heart would burst. He lay his head on the pillow next to him and let his Daddy's warm breath bathe him. 'I'm waiting for you Daddy,' he whispered. 'I'm always waiting …'

*

Over Three Years Later …

Buddy stirred in his sleep. He heard a whisper.
'Buddy. I'm here …'
He opened his eyes, raised his head and looked across a sea of sleeping Goldens. There were no Elves in the cottage. *I must be dreaming,* he thought. He lay down his head and closed his eyes and then he heard it again.
'Buddy, I'm outside.'
The voice was familiar. Something deep down inside him stirred. He stood up and carefully stepped through his sleeping friends and quietly pushed the door open. He stood on the veranda and looked across the meadow. A full moon hung in the sky over Rainbow Bridge like a huge glowing ball, casting its soft, luminous light over the meadows and lake. It was an eerily still night, no wind rustled the leaves in the trees and the lake was as calm as a millpond. The Rainbow Bridge landscape was peacefully quiet.
He peered into the dark and thought he saw someone walking towards him. His tail involuntarily rose and swished once from left to right. His heart started to race in his chest as the person stepped out into the moonlight. It couldn't be, surely. His tail wagged frantically as he realised who was walking towards him.
'My Daddy!' He ran towards the approaching man and almost jumped into his outstretched arms.
'Oh Buddy, it's so good to see you again. It broke my heart when you left us so young.'

But Buddy wasn't answering. He jumped up and down and manically licked his Daddy's face as his tail thrashed back and forth. Richard calmed Buddy down and knelt with him.

'You're looking well, Buddy. You were never far from my thoughts.'

Buddy didn't respond at first. He carefully studied his Daddy. He looked just as he remembered him. Thick grey hair swept back, his eyes sparkling, that soft voice. Oh, how he loved his Daddy. He rested his head against Richard's chest and listened to the beat of his heart as his Daddy wrapped his arms around him. Buddy loved being cuddled by his Daddy. Happy memories of his time at home came flooding back.

He lifted his head and looked deep into his Daddy's eyes, the pain was clear to see.

'Are you OK, Daddy?'

Richard tried to smile but his mouth wouldn't respond. 'I've been very ill, Buddy. I ... I'm like you now, on the next stage of my life journey.'

Buddy let the words sink in. 'So, you ... so you won't be going home to Mummy?'

Tears welled in Richard's eyes. 'Sadly not, Buddy. I won't be going home ever again.'

'But Daddy, how come you are here now? I thought you and Mummy would come for me, so we could climb the stone steps together.'

Richard cuddled Buddy close to him as the tears streamed down his face. 'I am very fortunate, Buddy. I met Daetia the Unicorn and Baelon the Guardian of Rainbow Bridge on my journey through the mist. They told me I could come to see you.'

Buddy's eyes opened wide with surprise and joy. 'Will you be able to come again? Oh Daddy, that would be wonderful.'

Richard smiled and dried his eyes. 'I'm not sure. I'm guessing anything is possible on Rainbow Bridge.'

'I wonder if the Chronicler is writing our story, Daddy.'

'I would say almost certainly,' said Richard. 'He wrote about you. His story gave me great comfort.'

Buddy looked at his Daddy, his eyes wide open in amazement. 'He wrote about me?'

'I asked him if he'd seen you on his visits. He told me you were one of the Pupstars, Buddy. I was so happy.'

Now Buddy was even more surprised. 'You know the Chronicler, Daddy?'

'He is a member of our Golden group. He walks among us and tells tales of our dogs on Rainbow Bridge. He brings great comfort to many, Buddy, especially to me when he wrote about you.'

'They say he walks among us too, Daddy, but nobody ever sees him. Except maybe for Baelon and Daetia. Maybe he will bring you with him on one of his visits?'

Richard's face lit up with a broad smile. 'I would love that.'

Buddy snuggled up close to Richard. 'Oh Daddy, so would I …'

*

Paddy's Day

A Short Story by Ian O'Neill

Paddy lay on top of the hill to the rear of the cottages, a spot that enjoyed a panoramic view across Rainbow Bridge. The flower covered stone steps loomed large and magnificent over the tranquil lake, alongside the rainbow that was its permanent companion. It was a place where he liked to enjoy the solitude of his own company and reflect on his life, usually after an action-packed day.

Paddy's day had been full of fun, frolics and adventure. In fact a typical day at the Bridge. He woke at eight in the morning and feasted on chicken and rice, one of his favourite meals. The Elves would give the dogs anything they wanted. Podge always had shoshages in the mornings which made his friends smile. Young Kevin had nicknamed him the Shoshage Dog which was quite novel considering he was a Golden Retriever!

After resting for an hour following their breakfast, they embarked on their first adventure of the day. Together with Brody, Rio, Darcy, Teal and Murphy, Paddy joined in the treasure trove that the Pixies organised in the forest. They hid treats and toys in the undergrowth for the dogs to find. They loved it, tails wagged, barks echoed all around the forest, and the Pixies would make it even more fun by hiding and jumping out on them.

Paddy found four bone shaped biscuits and a tennis ball. A Pixie threw the tennis ball into the undergrowth, and he bounded after it and emerged triumphantly, tail wagging, with it held firmly in his mouth. Then he dropped it on the ground at their feet before repeating the process. He never tired of it and what was better, neither did the Pixies.

Then the inevitable happened, the ball found its way into the murky pond deep in the heart of the forest. Was it by accident or was it deliberate? Only the Pixies knew for sure, but I know where my money lies. Paddy ran at full speed and dived into the thick, murky, green slime and grabbed the ball in his mouth. In a matter of seconds all his friends piled in with him. Mayhem ensued and around a dozen Goldies splashed and frolicked in the grime and the slime. They were ecstatic and quite possibly would have stayed there all morning when they heard a voice from the side of the pond.

'Oh, my, what have we here?' A tall Elf, long blond hair resting on his shoulders emerged from the dense undergrowth. He walked slowly over to the edge of the pond, his piercing, blue eyes sparkling like diamonds on a sunny day. The dogs stopped playing instantly and looked across to see Gladon smiling down at them. 'I wonder how you all ended up in here?'

The Pixies stood across the other side of the pond doing their best to look innocent. Gladon walked around the pond and crouched down in front of them. 'I don't suppose this has anything to do with you?'

They looked at each other before turning to the Elf and simultaneously shaking their heads.

'The tennis balls found their own way into the pond no doubt?'

The Pixies nodded.

Gladon burst into laughter. 'Well guys, let's get our Golden friends to the lake and see if we can wash some of this dirt off!'

Paddy and his mates jumped out of the pond and shook themselves - the black muck, green slime and water flew off them covering the Elf and Pixies. Gladon looked a picture, he was covered from head to foot in dark spots, like he was wearing a green polka dot jacket and pants!

'Come on you rascals,' he laughed, 'let's go back to the lake and get you cleaned up,' and he chased them through the forest followed by the Pixies.

As soon as they arrived back at the cottages, Paddy and his pals ran full pelt into the deep blue lake and swam out to meet their mates who were already there; Rumpole, Hitchcock, Buddy, Harry, Honey and Annie. The lake was clear blue and mirror calm when they arrived, but not for long. The Pixies and Gladon threw tennis balls in for them to swim and they left trails of mud and slime in the water. They were there for a good hour before running back to the cottages to dry their coats. The Elves wrapped them in warm towels and gave them chews to pass the time as they dried.

Paddy was planning to have a lazy afternoon and found a nice comfy bed by the blazing log fire, his favourite place to sleep. Well that was until Olly, Max, Toby, Harvey and Kevin persuaded him to join them.

'Who doesn't love a run and game in the Fields of Gold,' said Olly wagging his tail. 'Come on, Paddy, you know you want to!'

Paddy knew resistance was futile and dragged himself from his bed and trotted out of the cottage towards the golden field alongside the others. As they approached the barley, Harvey suddenly bolted full speed and disappeared into the tall golden stalks. He would always run right into the middle of the barley and hide, and it was up to the others to find him. They would chase him for hours and never tire. All an outside observer would see were wagging tails sticking out the top of the barley and the occasional furry head pop up. It was mighty fun characterised by the laughing and joyous barks.

So as the daylight faded, a tired Paddy lay sphinx-like on his own looking across Rainbow Bridge. His eyes were drawn to the golden arch on the far side of the lake and his mind would drift. It had been several years since he'd made that journey through the mist to be met by Daetia. His old life had stopped so suddenly and so cruelly without any warning. No farewell to his family, no preparation for the journey he was about to undertake. But Daetia, Baelon and his Elves along with his canine friends had helped him to slowly acclimatise to the changes.

He would sometimes imagine what he would say if he could write his Mummy a letter ...

'My Darling Mummy,

I've been thinking about you and decided to drop you a line. I am very happy here in Rainbow Bridge and have met some wonderful friends. The Elves really look after us well and the Pixies play with us all day, every day. I get to eat all my favourite food, and when we have chicken, we always get the skin. Mind you, Olly reckons the chicken must have been the size of an Elephant as every one of us gets a piece!

You would've laughed if you had seen me today, Mummy. I was covered in muddy dark slime when I came out of the pond. Gladon the Elf said I looked like a black Labrador and laughed when I shook myself because I covered him in dirty black spots. We all like Gladon, he is very kind to us, mind you, they all are. Baelon always seems to know when we're missing home and comes to cuddle us. As much as I love his cuddles, Mummy, there isn't anything I wouldn't give to have one of yours again.

All the dogs here are my friends, but I do have some special ones. Maisie and Sonny-Boy are like parents to us all, they listen to our problems and are always there to give us support. Toffee, the chocolate brown Labrador, is just so wise, she seems to understand what the Bridge is all about and spends many hours answering our questions. Olly is awesome and is always up to something. Baelon calls him the 'Master of Mischief'. He is just such fun to be around.

But Olly did help me recently. He told me how he'd been back to see his brothers and his Mummy. I didn't understand. He said, 'The last thing you think of before you go to sleep, Paddy, is your home and family. Think of your Mummy and Daddy and your brothers or sisters, then you will dream of them. And when you dream of them you are with them.'

And that's what I did, Mummy, and there you were. I watched you as you slept. I rested my head on your pillow and kissed you. Oh Mummy, I can't tell you how happy it made me. And now I know how to, I will always come back.

Well, Mummy, Gladon has just sounded the gong for our supper. Shoshages and mash for me tonight with lovely thick gravy. Please don't worry about me, I am happy here. I will wait here for you until that special day when I see you emerge through that golden arch and I leap into your arms. And then, we will cross the Bridge together.

Think of me often as I will think of you...
Your ever-loving special Golden boy, Paddy.'

*

Jackson's Birthday

A Short Story by Ian O'Neill

The two Goldens ran across the lush green meadow like only Goldens can. Tails flying high like sails, ears flapping, their soft coats flattened by the rushing wind. First one led, then the other. There was no let up until they arrived at the top of the rolling hill far to the west of their cottages. They both threw themselves onto the grass and rolled onto their backs, moaning and groaning with delight.

'You're slowing up in your old age, little bro,' said Jake.

'It's been a while since I had a good run through the fields. But don't worry, I'll be giving you a serious run when I'm fully fit,' smiled Jackson.

Both Goldens finished their rolling and lay on their fronts, front paws crossed, in the sphinx position. Their ears flapped, their noses twitched, and their eyes searched their surroundings.

'Rainbow Bridge is beautiful,' said Jackson.

'It is indeed,' agreed Jake. 'I've been discovering new places ever since I arrived.'

The two brothers sat quietly for several moments taking in the views. It had only been a few days since Jackson arrived and he was still coming to terms with the huge changes in his life. All new arrivals to the Bridge struggled at first. The wrench of leaving their families had a huge emotional impact on them and it would take time for them to acclimatise.

'I'm glad you're here with me,' said Jackson turning to his brother.

Jake reached across and tenderly touched Jackson's paw. 'Always here for you little bro.'

Jackson nodded and looked out across the rolling hills towards a wood in the distance. He remembered all the walks with his Mummies and Skye, and then in the last couple of years with little Freddie. How he loved his sister and brother. And he loved the holidays they shared. Beach walking and watching his sister and brother play in the sea. He was on holiday when he knew that it was his time. A tear formed in the corner of his eye and trickled slowly down his nose.

'It's OK to feel a little lost during the early days here,' said Jake. 'We all feel the same when we first arrive. It's a big change to what we were used to. We come from a loving home, Jackson. Our Mummies are the best. They took care of all our needs. I still remember the hugs and snuggles with them.'

More tears flowed from Jackson's eyes. The last thing he remembers was the grieving tears of his two Mummies as he peacefully drifted off to sleep. He wanted to say to them, 'Don't worry, Mummies, I am ready for this.' But that was the last he heard from them as he walked slowly through the mist.

Jake jumped up. 'Come on little bro, I'll race you to the wood!'

With that he sped off down the hill. Jackson was soon up and running after his brother. It felt good to feel the wind on his face again. His legs no longer ached from arthritis. His front legs stretched out in front of him as his back legs propelled him forwards. His mouth was wide open as he gulped in mouthfuls of air, long pink tongue hanging out of the side of his mouth. It looked like he was laughing, and he was, laughing with every ounce of his being.

Running is freedom!

Jackson caught up with Jake just as they entered the wood, and they didn't let up. Racing each other along the paths; jumping over tree roots, running through the bracken and ferns, before finally splashing in the pond! The two dogs emerged soaking wet. A synchronised shake quickly followed before they threw themselves down on a patch of grass.

'That was awesome,' said Jackson. 'I'd forgotten just how exhilarating a good run can be.'

'That's the first thing I noticed when I arrived,' said

Jake. 'I felt like a young dog again. No more pains in my back or legs and I could breathe easily. Rainbow Bridge really is a magical place.'

'I'm beginning to realise that,' smiled Jackson.

'I have made some true friendships since I've been here,' said Jake. 'We're all desperately sad that we've been separated from our families but there is such great camaraderie between us all. If you're ever feeling down, I'm always here for you, but there are many others too. Maisie is a great listener, and Max, Toby, Sonny and Rory. There are many others too. And if you need cheering up, Podge will always be there offering you a shoshage, or you can chase Olly through the Fields of Gold. Please don't ever suffer in silence, little bro.'

Jackson smiled. 'I'm so glad I have you as my big bro. You've always looked out for me.'

'And I always will.'

Jake jumped up. 'Come on, little bro, we've got more places to explore.' And the two brothers ran off through the undergrowth barking their delight!

The day was spent running through woods and forests, splashing in ponds and streams, running through meadows and up and down rolling hills or lying down in the sun and chatting. And as the two brothers slowly walked back to their cottage they heard the welcome sound of the supper gong in the distance.

'I don't know about you, little bro, but I'm starving. I could eat a feathered Ostrich!'

Jackson burst into laughter. 'Where did you get that saying from?'

'It's one of Olly's many sayings. He keeps us all entertained.'

As they neared the cottages, Jackson noticed all the dogs were assembled outside. They surrounded a small group of the Elves.

'Why aren't they inside eating their supper?'

'They're probably waiting for their bowls to be put out' said Jake.

'But all the Goldies usually run inside as soon as they hear the gong,' said Jackson looking across at Jake.

'I'm sure there's a good reason why,' said Jake not holding Jackson's stare.

The two brothers slowly walked up to the gathered Goldies and just as they reached them, the assembled dogs parted followed by the Elves, revealing a table with a huge cake on top of it, covered in burning candles. Baelon was crouching behind the table and said, 'After three, one – two - three – And they all shouted, 'Happy Birthday, Jackson!'

Jackson looked at Jake, surprise didn't cover what he felt at that moment.

Jake leant across and kissed Jackson on his nose. 'Happy Birthday, little bro!'

Three young Goldies ran up to Jackson, their tails frantically wagging.

'Jackson, you've got to blow out the candles,' they screamed.

He walked up to the table and took a long, slow in-breath …

'And don't forget to make a wish!' said Little Sausage, jumping up and down like a baby kangaroo!

Jackson hesitated for a second before blowing with all his might across the flaming cake and extinguishing all the candles in one go. The young dogs shouted, 'Hurrah!' as they all gathered round him to sing a rousing chorus of 'Happy Birthday'.

'Can we cut the cake?' said a bouncing Honeybee as soon as they finished.

Baelon produced a knife and sliced the huge cake up into even portions and placed the wedges into their individual bowls.

'It's a shoshage cake,' beamed Podge. 'With cream cheese, carrots and peanut butter!'

The next few minutes were relatively quiet as the assembled Goldens ravenously ate their cake, accompanied by the sound of ringing tags as they licked every last morsel from their bowls.

Cries of, 'Speech,' rang around the pack as Jackson stepped back from his bowl. He looked nervously at Jake, who nodded his encouragement.

He coughed to clear his throat and hesitantly started to speak. 'Er … I'm not very good at this. I've been letting Jake do most of my talking since I arrived.'

Jake stood next to him and whispered words of encouragement in his ear. 'Go on, little bro, just say what you feel.'

Jackson took another long breath and looked around at all the expectant Goldies surrounding him. The young ones at the front wagging their tails excitedly.

'Thank you all for my birthday wishes. What an amazing surprise.' He turned to Jake and smiled. 'I wonder how you all knew?'

The Goldies all looked at Jake and chuckled as Jake did his best to look innocent.

'The cake was delicious.' He looked across to Podge. 'I think that is the first shoshage cake I've ever had! It's been a wonderful day with my brother. He showed me all around Rainbow Bridge and I rediscovered the wonder of running through fields, woods and streams again, something we did together many times in our past. I thank you all for being so helpful and welcoming since I arrived, and I want to thank the Elves for looking after me. It's my first birthday away from home and I want to thank you all from the bottom of my heart for making it so special.'

All the Goldies ran around barking and wagging their tails. It was a sight to behold, and a great birthday party ensued. They played games, namely: find the shoshage, chase the Goldie, (Olly), catch the treat, pull the rope tuggy, dunk the plastic duck, plus many, many more. It was a party Jackson would remember for ever.

At the end of the day, the tired Goldies trooped one by one into the cottages and slumped into their beds. It was no surprise to find they were exhausted after an exciting day.

Jackson and Jake were the last two and lay outside looking across the grass towards the lake.

'Thanks for making it such a special day for me, Jake.'

'You're welcome, little bro.'

'It's my first birthday without our Mummies,' said Jackson sadly.

Jake reached across and gently rested his paw on top of Jackson's. 'We had some great birthdays together, didn't we little bro. Our Mummies always made them so special.'

'Can I tell you something,' said Jackson.

'You can tell me anything,' said Jake.

'When were out today, running across the meadows, I thought I heard someone singing Happy Birthday to me.' He turned to Jake. 'It sounded like our Mummies.'

A knowing smile spread across Jake's lips. 'I would bet my last Bonio it was our Mummies. They would want you to know that they're celebrating your special day, little bro.'

Tears glistened Jackson's eyes. 'I knew they wouldn't forget.'

'Come on, little bro, time for bed. I'm shattered.' Jake dragged himself to his feet, leant over and kissed Jackson on his head. 'Happy Birthday, Jackson, I love you, mate.'

Jackson looked up to Jake. 'And I love you too …'

As Jake walked into the cottage, Jackson stood and looked up at the full moon as it rested directly over the Bridge, its luminescent white light reflected in the blue lake, sparkling like precious jewels across its surface. Jackson thought it looked beautiful. He smiled to himself. He could see Mummy Bev with her camera taking photographs. A happy memory among many happy memories.

Happiness and sadness conflicted inside him as he thought back to the wonderful life he shared with Mummy Pen and Mummy Bev. If he could've chosen a life, he would've chosen his life. It was full of love and laughter. What more could a Goldie want?

As he walked into the cottage, he hesitated and looked up at the full moon and whispered, 'Goodnight Mummy Pen, goodnight Mummy Bev. Thank you both for being my Mummies. I was truly honoured to be your special boy. Look for the signs as they are there. Especially when we are missing each other the most. And remember in those special moments, Jackson's close …'

*

Finlay

A Short Story by Ian O'Neill

Murph's Diary one week after arriving at Rainbow Bridge.

So, Paddy B has me up early in the morning. It's a week after I arrived at the Bridge. Paddy being the good sort he is recognised that I was feeling low and decided that I needed a run through the fields and forests. So off we set at the crack of dawn and ran. It's taken a few days to get used to the lack of the aul arthritis as me legs no longer ache, and I can run like a one year old again.

We ran through meadows, up hills, down hills, through forests, splashed in streams and eventually finished up by throwing ourselves onto the lush grass at the top of a hill.

'That was grand,' sez I.

'And how are you feeling?' asks Paddy.

'Much better, thanks to you, me aul mate.'

'What are friends for?' sez Paddy.

It was then that Paddy noticed a lone Goldie trotting through the field below us. He sprang to his feet and said, 'Let's catch up with them and see if they would like a run with us.'

Well Paddy was off like a hungry dog at dinner time and sprinted down the hill. I jumped up and sped after him. We caught up with the Goldie in seconds flat and I think we may have surprised him as he stopped in his tracks and looked like a frightened rabbit. Paddy and I put the brakes on and pulled up a matter of inches in front of him.

'It's alright, young fella,' sez I. 'We just thought you might like a run with us.'

He didn't answer and instead lowered his gaze.

'You're new here aren't you?' sez Paddy.

The Goldie nodded.

'What's your name?' I asked.

'Finlay, or Fin.'

'Welcome, Fin. I'm Murph and this is Paddy.'

Then Paddy surprises me.

'I'm sure I know you,' sez Paddy. 'Didn't we meet at an IRR reunion?'

Finlay looked up and for the first time his face broke into a smile. 'My Mummy's names is Yvette; my Daddy's name is Tim and my brother's called Marlow.'

'I was there with me big sis, Lexie, and me little bro, Theo,' sez Paddy.

'Jeez, Paddy,' sez I, 'I'm beginning to think you know every dog in England!'

'Come on, Fin,' sez Paddy, 'there's a small wood over the hill and there's a stream that we can all splash in.'

Well our Fin's face lit up when he heard there was a stream and three of us ran like the wind over the hill and down towards the wood and the young fella jumped into the stream and splashed around like a young pup. It was great fun. And when we finally ran out of energy and we found a nice thick patch of grass and rolled like mad things to dry ourselves off.

It was pawsome!

'Well,' sez Paddy, 'and how are you both feeling now?'

'Brilliant,' says Fin.

'Grand,' sez I.

'You see,' sez Paddy, 'we all feel lost sometimes, especially so when we first arrive here. But a brisk run and play with your friends, soon has you feeling happy again.'

'I'm missing my Mummy and Daddy, and Marlow,' sez Finlay.

Jeez I felt sad for him. I rested me paw on top of the young fella's. 'I know the feeling. I've only been here a week meself.'

'What you'll both learn is that we're all here for each other,' sez Paddy. 'We all have our down days, but the others soon rally round and cheer you up. And there's young Olly and his Pupstars. They love meeting the new arrivals.'

Fin smiled. 'He took me to the Fields of Gold as soon as I arrived.'

'Olly sees it as his role to make everyone happy,' sez

Paddy.

'And he does it well,' sez I.

'It's just …' Fin's words trailed off and his sad look returned.

'It's OK, Fin lad,' sez I. 'We're all here for you. Any time you need to talk, just look for me or Paddy. We're great listeners.'

'I woke in the middle of the night. I didn't know where I was. I looked for Marlow and my Mummy and Daddy. And then I remembered I was at Rainbow Bridge. I miss them all so much.'

The tears misted his eyes. Me aul heart ached for him.

'Now, I had a similar experience the first week I was here,' sez I. 'I expected to see me Mammy and Daddy, and Luce and Henry when I woke in the night. It made me pine for home. I spoke to Baelon the next day. Now that lovely fella is a wise aul soul. He told me that when we're with our families, we embed them into our hearts, and they do the same with us. So when the day comes we have to leave them, it hurts us to our core. It's like we've left something behind.

But the reality is that we take a piece of their hearts with us and leave a piece of our own hearts with them. I found it so comforting to think that a part of them is still with me.'

I sat up and patted me chest with me paw. 'Your Mammy, Daddy and Marlow are safe and sound with you, young Fin. And that's where they'll always be.'

The young fella's face broke into a smile. 'That makes me feel so much better,' sez he.

'I'm glad,' sez I.

'And speak to them when you have a moment on your own,' sez Paddy. 'They're always listening.'

'And when you dream of them, you really are with them,' sez I. 'And you can rest assured, they'll be dreaming of you.'

Just at that moment we hear the gong sound in the distance. It was breakfast time.

'Come on,' sez Paddy, 'let's run back before the others

eat it all!'

With that, the three of us sped off up the hill back towards the cottages. It was just another day on Rainbow Bridge where pals do what they do best. Take care of each other.

Slainté Murph.

*

Fudge's Message Home

A Short Story by Ian O'Neill

Fudge looked a sad and forlorn figure as she sat alone alongside the Fields of Gold. She gazed out across Rainbow Bridge from her vantage point on top of the hill. The fading sun cast its shallow light across the landscape as the day drew slowly to its end. It was a time of day that she would normally look forward to following full-on Goldie play with her friends in the lakes, the forests, and the Fields of Gold.

She was one of Olly's pupstars and loved her young friends. Their bond being the sudden and tragic circumstances of their early separations from their hooman families. Olly was their leader and ensured that each and every day was fun, and action packed. He never gave them time to dwell too much on their sadness. Fudge, Kevin, Buddy, Zoe and Bonnie would follow Olly to the ends of Rainbow Bridge and back.

But tonight, Fudge needed to be on her own and Olly sensed that and watched with the others as she walked slowly up the hill. She sat down and stared across the blue lake towards the golden arch and her mind drifted back to her life with her two Mummies. She'd felt lucky that she got to live with her canine Mummy and her human Mummy but that's where her lucky feeling ended. She felt robbed that she got to spend so little time with them both.

Fudge had been ill for as long as she could remember and her hooman Mummy had worked hard with the Healers to cure her of her condition but sadly it wasn't to be. In the end she was just too weak and started on her journey to Rainbow Bridge as her Mummy's grieving tears echoed in her ears.

Oh how she missed her hooman Mummy. Her life, as short as it was, was full of love and fun. Her Mummy adored her and she in turn adored her Mummy. She spent all of her time with her two Mummies, walking in green fields, running through woods and forests and the best of all, running along the sand and splashing in the sea. What would she give for one more walk with them? Anything.

Her thoughts were interrupted by a rustle from the golden barley behind her. A handsome head followed by a giant, curly body and paws the size of a lion slowly emerged. It was of course Harvey.

'Oh Fudge, you startled me! I didn't expect to see anyone up here at this time. Why aren't you having your supper with the others?'

'I'm not feeling that hungry tonight,' she said sadly.

Harvey looked puzzled. 'We're Golden Retrievers – we're always hungry!'

As much as she tried, Fudge couldn't force a smile. Instead she burst into tears. Harvey wrapped her in his giant paws and held her close. 'Oh Fudge, what is it?'

The words wouldn't come as Fudge sobbed gently into his furry coat. Harvey hugged her tightly and kissed her head. 'Weep little one, let your sadness flow away with your tears.'

When Fudge eventually calmed down, Harvey released her and kissed her nose. He sat down next to her and said, 'I'm always here, Fudge, if you need to talk. And you have so many friends here who want to help. Maisie is a great listener and will always lend a sympathetic ear.'

Fudge wiped her eyes with her paw and tried her best to smile. 'But she has Bambi and Cody to look after. She doesn't need me burdening her with my troubles too.'

Harvey leant across and looked directly into her deep brown eyes. 'Now listen here, young lady, let me tell you that our Maisie has a heart the size of Rainbow Bridge and she would never turn anyone away who needs a friendly ear.'

Fudge's tears started to flow again. 'It's just … It's just that I miss home so much. I miss my Mummies. It was always the three of us and we went everywhere together. I feel as if I have had my heart wrenched from my body. I loved them so much. Why did it have to end so soon?'

Harvey sighed deeply. 'Oh Fudge, I wish I could answer

that question. It breaks my heart to see you young pups arriving here. I know how fortunate I was to live for fifteen years with my Mummy. I had all the love in the world which is why I have plenty to share with you young ones.' He wrapped her in his giant paws again. 'It would've broken your Mummy's heart to have to let you go so young. But she couldn't bear to see you suffering which is why she took the heart-breaking decision to let you go. She must love you very much, little Fudge.'

Harvey kissed her nose then gently licked away her tears. Fudge forced a smile and looked up at him with her deep brown, soulful eyes. 'Thanks, Harvey, you are so kind. I think I just needed to let the sadness out.'

Harvey smiled and ruffled her head. 'That's exactly what it is. We all feel sad at times, little one.'

Fudge smiled for the first time. 'I love it when you call me little one. My Mummy used to call me the Fudgester.'

'It's the hooman way,' said Harvey. 'I was Curlywurlycuddlebumptious!'

Fudge laughed out loud. 'Oh Harvey, that is wonderful. Who named you that?'

'My Mummy's friends at the Golden meets. And it was my Auntie April who called me Lionpaws.' He held up his right paw. 'I'm sure you can guess why!'

Fudge laughed again, a delicious infectious giggle.

'Now that's more like it, young Fudge. You have the most beautiful smile when you laugh.'

Fudge leant over and kissed Harvey on his nose. 'Thank you, Harvey. You are a wonderful friend to me.'

Harvey looked embarrassed. 'I'm here to help,' he said modestly.

'Can I ask you a question, Harvey?'

'Of course.'

'I've heard the others talk of a Chronicler who writes about Rainbow Bridge. Do you know who this person is?'

Harvey looked thoughtfully at her. 'I too have heard of this person. I'm told he walks among us.'

'Is he an Elf?' asked Fudge.

'I don't think so,' said Harvey.

They both sat quietly for several minutes.

'Do you think he knows about our conversation?'

'Quite possibly. Why do you ask?'

'I would love to send a message home to my two Mummies.'

'What do you want to say?' asked Harvey.

Fudge thought for a moment. 'I love and miss you Mummy Pauline and Mummy Pippa. I want you to know that I long for that time we can be together again but that I am happy at Rainbow Bridge with the best friends a young Golden Retriever could ever wish for. I want you both to be well and to enjoy all those things that we used to do. And to always think of me when you do them. Love you Mummies with all my heart, your darling little Fudgester.'

Tears misted Harvey's eyes. 'I think they will love that.' He leant over and tenderly kissed her nose.

They sat quietly for several moments before Harvey stood up. 'Come on, young lady, supper is waiting and I'm starving.'

Fudge jumped up beside him. 'Me too!'

The two Goldens trotted off down the hill happily chatting.

'I hope it's chicken tonight,' said Fudge.

'Me too,' said Harvey. 'With lots of skin!'

'We all manage to get a big piece of skin with our chicken,' said Fudge. 'Olly says that the chicken must be the size of an elephant!'

'He does indeed,' laughed Harvey.

*

Maggie May

A Short Story by Ian O'Neill

Baelon stepped out onto the veranda and watched the dogs playing on the grass in front of the cottages. It was a familiar after breakfast scene, but it never failed to fill his heart with joy. As long as the dogs were happy then his job was a success. Olly and his Pupstars were running up the hill behind the cottages towards the Fields of Gold and he'd persuaded Harvey and Podge to join them. And another group swam in the blue lake under the bridge. He thought he would overflow with happiness.

But then his eye caught a lone dog sat upon the hill in the distance staring towards the golden arch. She'd arrived three days ago and had barely interacted with the other dogs. She showed little interest in food and would spend her days sitting in the same spot. He had learned over the years that all dogs reacted differently following their arrival on Rainbow Bridge, but this girl bothered him. The Healers and the Carers were unable to reach her. He decided that he would spend the day with her, even if they sat in the same spot the whole time.

He slowly walked up the hill and as he approached she didn't even notice him such was her focus on the arch. 'Good morning young Maggie. Would you mind if I joined you?'

She looked up at him with sad eyes but didn't respond before turning her attention back to the arch.

'Many of the dogs like to look at the arch,' said Baelon. 'It helps them remember home. All the dogs here miss home terribly, but they learn to enjoy the beautiful conditions here and more importantly, to enjoy each other's company. You really can make some wonderful friends here, Maggie.'

She turned to him, her dark eyes misted with tears. 'I want to go home. I miss my Mummy and my brothers and sisters.'

He knelt down beside her and gently rubbed her head and back. 'If it was in my power I would gladly take you back home, young Maggie, but you were very ill before you left the human world. Rainbow Bridge is healing you ready for the next part of your journey when the time comes. And in the future your brothers and sisters will join you. And it is here where you will all wait for your Mummy.'

'Will Millie come here too?'

He hugged her. 'Yes of course when it's her time.'

She turned back to the arch. Baelon jumped back to his feet. 'Come, young Maggie, walk with me around the lake. I've yet to meet a Golden Retriever that doesn't love to walk around clear blue water. Although on reflection, you may prefer the muddy variety to swim in!'

She looked up at him and he was sure he saw a trace of a smile cross her lips. She slowly stood up and walked alongside Baelon down the hill towards the lake. She didn't speak but Baelon knew from experience that he had to take it slowly with this precious girl. She would speak when she was ready.

They approached a wooden bench by the lake's edge and Baelon said, 'come, young Maggie, let us sit here together and let the calm of the blue water relax us as we watch the others play.'

Maggie jumped up onto the bench next to Baelon as he sat down and leant against him. He put his arm around her and they both looked out onto the lake and let the tranquillity bathe them. They didn't speak for a while but that was OK, as the Elf knew the lake had healing powers and would soothe her fears.

'I used to live near the sea,' she said.

'What a wonderful place to live, young Maggie. There is something uplifting about living close to the sea.'

'We would all go to the beach together sometimes,' she said. 'There were six of us.'

'A big pack indeed,' said Baelon.

'Sometimes we would meet other dogs and walk with them. Oh Baelon, it was such fun. And my Mummy Louise, she …' Tears trickled down her face.

'That's OK, Maggie. It's going to hurt for a while. You have wonderful memories; you will learn to treasure them.'

'My Mummy Louise was so patient with Millie and me. Our lives were not good before.'

'Your Mummy is special indeed,' said Baelon. 'Human Carers have the same dedication as their Elven counterparts on Rainbow Bridge.'

Maggie stared out across the still lake seemingly lost in special memories. 'I will never forget her, Baelon.'

He smiled warmly and patted her chest. 'This is where your Mummy is safely stored, as you are stored safely in her heart. It is a bond that is unbreakable.'

'Will I have to wait long before I see her again?' she asked.

The Elf leant close and whispered in her ear. 'One of our dogs met his Mummy on this bench only two days ago.'

Maggie's eyes opened wide in amazement. 'But how did she come here?'

'Rainbow Bridge is magic, Maggie, anything is possible.'

Maggie's whole demeanour lifted at the thought of seeing her Mummy again. 'How will she know where I am? There are so many dogs here.'

'There is a human who walks among us,' said Baelon mysteriously. 'He is known as the Rainbow Bridge Chronicler in the human world. He will write your story, I'm sure.'

Maggie jumped off the bench and ran around in circles wagging her tail and barking with glee. 'Oh Baelon, that makes me so happy that my Mummy knows where I am.'

A broad smile spread across Baelon's face. 'So young Maggie, can I interest you in some breakfast?'

Maggie stopped running around and looked up at him with her huge brown eyes. 'Oh yes please. One of the dogs offered me a shoshage last night and I turned it down. I wish I hadn't now.'

Baelon sprang to his feet and said, 'Shoshages it is. Let's head back to the cottages.'

The two of them walked back towards the cottages happily chatting. 'Was it Podge who offered you the shoshage?' he asked.

'I'm not sure,' said Maggie. 'He was very handsome though. He said that shoshages cure all known ills.'

'That's our Podge,' laughed Baelon. 'And who am I to doubt such wisdom?'

Maggie laughed so hard she started to bark. Rainbow Bridge had worked its magic once again.

*

Gracie-Baby

A Short Story by Ian O'Neill

Two Golden Retrievers ran like the wind across an open meadow. A third ran several metres behind but was gaining ground fast. Many who read this will have had the pleasure of watching their Goldens in full flight. They run like racehorses in a classic race. Legs stretching out front and behind, eating up the green turf below their feet. It truly is a sight to marvel at.

But the race to Willow's Pond was a serious affair and the three pals ran for all their worth.

'Quick! She's catching us, Olly.'

'Don't worry, Kevin, she's running out of ground. The pond is just over the hill.'

But as they approached the brow of the hill, the chasing Goldie caught up and then overtook them and ran full speed at the pond until the grass ran out and she landed with an almighty splash on her belly, quickly followed by Olly and Kevin. Then Goldie mayhem commenced. They ran around, jumped on each other, splashed, barked, played bitey face, until they were all exhausted and then flopped on the grass next to the pond.

'Well, Gracie, I have to give you full marks for catching us,' said Olly panting.

Little Kevin stood up and shook himself, covering the other two in a shower of muddy water.

'Thanks Kevin,' said a laughing Olly, 'as if we weren't already wet enough.'

'Got to be done,' said Kevin, 'it's part of Goldie law.'

'Who told you that?' asked Olly.

'You did!' smiled Kevin as he had a roll on the grass to dry himself off.

Gracie replicated Kevin's shake and showered her two friends before joining Kevin with a manic roll on the grass. Once she finished, they all lay face down looking across the meadow that stretched for as far as the eye could see.

'I love it here,' said Gracie. 'It's so peaceful.'

'Me too,' agreed Olly.

'What, more than the Fields of Gold?'

Olly pondered her question for a few seconds. 'I love them both but for different reasons,' answered Olly diplomatically.

'I love all of Rainbow Bridge,' said Kevin. 'If my Mummy and Henry were here then it would be just perfect.'

Olly nodded his agreement, but Gracie was quiet and seemed lost in her thoughts.

'What is it Gracie? You're very quiet,' said Olly.

'It's three years to the day that I arrived here. I'm missing my Mummy and my brothers and sisters.'

'I'm really sorry,' said Olly, 'I didn't realise.'

'That's OK, Olly,' said Gracie. 'I love it here, especially being a Pupstar and playing with you all, but today I'm thinking about home.'

'We do understand,' said Olly. 'Anniversaries are meant to be about remembering home, especially the hoomans and dogs we've left behind.'

'I used to love us all going out together, running in the fields and forests but I especially used to love the beaches. Miles of sand, sea and surf. What fun we had jumping in and out of the waves.'

'I used to chase my brother, Bennie through a golden field. It was the best,' said Olly.

Kevin and Gracie looked at him. 'So that's why you love the fields of golden barley.'

Olly looked momentarily sad. 'I can't describe to you how it felt. When I run in the Fields of Gold here it reminds me of those carefree times.'

Gracie and Kevin both reached across and rested a paw on top of his, but in typical Olly style the smile soon returned. 'But it's your day today, Gracie, so, we'll play on the beach.'

'But, Olly, there are no beaches on Rainbow Bridge,' said Gracie.

'Well,' said Olly, 'according to Baelon, all we have to do is to wish with all of our hearts and we can create any landscape we wish.'

'But, Olly, a beach!' said Gracie.

'Why not?' said Olly jumping up. 'Come on guys, stand with me.'

The three pals stood side by side. 'Right,' said Olly, 'Close your eyes and imagine a beach over the far hill. Imagine miles of golden sands and the waves from the sea crashing over us as we play.'

They all closed their eyes and wished. Gracie concentrated as hard as she could to the point where she could swear she smelt the sea.

'Right,' said Olly, 'Let's go, race you to the beach!'

And the three pals sped off. A feeling of anticipation swept over Gracie, a feeling that she hadn't felt for a long, long time. *Oh, to play on a beach again.* And as she approached the brow of the hill she swore she could hear the sea. Surely not, it couldn't be? But when she reached the top of the hill she stopped. Her breath momentarily left her as she stared out across the miles of golden sand that stretched out before her as far as her eyes could see. And the sound of the waves crashing onto the beach was like music to her soul.

Kevin and Olly stood either side of her, mouths wide open.

'Oh my,' said Kevin, 'I've never seen the sea before.'

'Me neither,' said Olly.

'It's … it's breath-taking,' said Kevin.

'It certainly is,' agreed Olly.

Tears misted Gracie's eyes as the memories came flooding back to her. Happy times playing with her siblings and friends.

'What are we waiting for?' said Olly.

And the three pals ran together across the golden sands and headed directly for the sea. They ran into the raging water and momentarily disappeared under the crashing waves, then three soggy Retrievers emerged, jumping up like salmon in a fast-flowing river.

'Wow!' said Olly, 'this is amazing!'

'I love it!' said Kevin.

Gracie ran through the surf, barking so hard she thought her voice would give out. It was just as she remembered it. Exhilarating, frightening, liberating. She felt free.

I'm not sure how long they played for, but the sun was setting to the west of them when Olly suggested it was time to go back to the cottages. Three soaking wet but very happy Retrievers trotted back across the beach. Once they reached the brow of the hill, they turned as one and watched as the beach and the sea slowly melted back into the landscape.

'Oh Olly,' said Gracie, 'that was magical.' She leant across and kissed his nose. 'Thank you for arranging this for me.'

Olly smiled. 'It's not me, Gracie. It's the magic of Rainbow Bridge.'

And with that the three friends trotted happily through the meadow. Olly and Kevin discussed what they were having for their tea while Gracie stayed within her own thoughts. She thought of her Mummy and told her all about her day.

Mummy, it's three years since I left you. A day doesn't pass where I don't think of you and my brothers and sisters, about all the fun times we had. The best times were on the beach where we all ran like mad things through the waves. Well, guess what Mummy? Me and my friends, Olly and Kevin found a beach on Rainbow Bridge today and we played just like we used to. I've had a brilliant day, Mummy. The only thing missing for me was you. Remember me the next time you're on the beach and imagine your little 'wrecking ball' creating havoc amongst the waves. I miss you every day, Mummy and I'm always thinking of you. Until that day we meet again, sending you all my love. Please give my brothers and sisters a big kiss from me. Yours, Gracie-Baby, your very own 'wrecking ball'.

Rainbow Olly

A Short Story by Ian O'Neill

When Max had finished his breakfast, he trotted out of the cottage and over to the meadow. He sat down next to his bro Toby. 'Where's our little hurricane this morning? He's normally first up for breakfast and first out into the fields.'

'I haven't seen him,' said Toby.

Sonny sat down next to them. 'I saw him walking up the hill towards the golden fields earlier. He was quiet and subdued which isn't like our Olly.'

Toby and Max exchanged concerned looks, when the penny dropped. 'I think we'd better find him,' said Max.

The two brothers jumped up and ran towards the hill to the rear of the cottages that overlooked Rainbow Bridge. It was as they approached the brow of the hill they saw their little brother lying on his front staring across the blue lake towards the golden arch. It was the place where Goldens went to when they sought solace. A place for quiet reflection.

Toby hesitated for a moment. 'Do you think we should leave him on his own for a while?'

'We can only ask the question,' said Max. 'If he wants time on his own he'll tell us.'

As they approached Olly he turned to them, a trace of a smile crossed his lips. 'It's so peaceful up here.'

Max and Toby lay down either side of him.

'It certainly is,' said Toby.

'We were wondering where you were. Sonny told us you were headed up here. We just wanted to …'

'I knew you'd find me. My two big bros always looking out for me.'

'We can go if you'd prefer,' said Max.

Olly turned towards him; Max saw the sadness clouding his eyes. 'I'd like you to stay.'

The three brothers sat quietly for a while looking out

across the blue lake under the shadow of the flower covered stone bridge, their eyes drawn towards the golden arch. Their old lives lay beyond that gateway. Lives that were still fresh in their minds.

'What do you miss most about home?' asked Olly.

'Being part of a family. They were always laughing and joking,' said Toby.

'Playing games with our Mummy and Daddy, and Cat and Vicky,' said Max.

'Would it surprise you if I said the Fields of Gold,' smiled Olly.

His two brothers had broad grins on their faces. 'Not much,' laughed Max.

'Something magical happened when Bennie and I ran through those fields. We ran and ran and never tired. I remember Mummy and Cat giggling away as they watched us. I never wanted those times to end.'

'I know little bro,' said Max laying his paw on top of Olly's.

'I feel ... I feel I was robbed of something special,' sighed Olly. Tears welled in his eyes. 'I still don't understand why it all had to end so suddenly.'

'What happened to you was cruel, little bro,' said Max. 'Toby was also taken too soon. But let me tell you something, Olly, no matter how long you get to stay with our Mummy and Daddy it is never enough. There isn't a day that goes by that I don't think of them all. I wish more than anything that we could all be together, and one day we will. But that is out of our hands. As Baelon often says, 'The vagaries of life will always remain a mystery.'

'And you Olly, of all the dogs on Rainbow Bridge, you embrace this place, this magical place and squeeze every last drop of joy that there is to be found here. I sometimes wonder who the big brother is, as it is you who lifts us all on our down days. But you need this time to grieve; you need to look after you, and you need to know that Toby and I will always be here for you. If you want to talk, we'll listen, if you want to sit here quietly, we'll sit with you. And if you want to cry, then little bro, we will cry with you.'

Tears flowed freely down Olly's face. 'How lucky am I to have such wonderful brothers? Bennie and Bailey at home and you two here to look after me. So many of our friends here have nobody. It just makes me so sad.'

'That's just it,' said Toby. 'They have you, little bro. They adore you. Zoe, Kevin, Buddy, Bonnie. You're always there for them. Listening, helping, encouraging, playing. You're the one they look up to Olly. You're their big bro.'

Olly laughed as he wiped his face on his paw. 'I think I get into too much mischief to ever be that. I can hear Mummy's voice in my head. 'Oh Olly, what have you done this time?' The tears flowed freely again. 'Whenever I was ill I would lose consciousness, I'm not sure how long for, but when I came round everything was fuzzy and I would have a raging headache, but our Mummy was always there. Caring, soothing, reassuring. What would you give for just one more cuddle with her?'

'Anything,' said Max.

'Me too,' said Toby.

Olly wiped his face on his front paw again and forced a smile. 'I can't believe it's been a year.'

'Where does the time go?' agreed Toby.

Olly stood, shook his head vigorously and took a long deep breath. Max and Toby stood alongside him and they both nuzzled him. 'We're always here for you little bro,' said Max.

Olly forced a tearful smile. 'I know, what would I do without my two big brothers?'

'Would you like a run in the fields?' asked Toby.

Olly shook his head. 'Maybe later. I know what I would like though.'

'Go on,' said Max.

'Shoshages - I haven't had any breakfast!'

'I'm sure Baelon will be very happy to arrange some,' said Toby.

'With gravy?'

'What else?' said Max.

The three brothers trotted back down the hill and although an air of sadness surrounded them, there was that ever-present aura of hope that followed Olly everywhere. He looked towards the arch and felt the familiar ache in his heart. Life had dealt him a cruel blow at such a young age but our Olly, although down, would always bounce back. His family had given him the values that would sustain him through his time on Rainbow Bridge, until that magical day when they were all back where they should be. Together again.

*

Lennie's Letter Home.

A Short Story by Ian O'Neill

My Dearest Mummy,

I wanted to let you know that I have arrived safely on Rainbow Bridge and have made many new friends. I met the most beautiful Unicorn called Daetia at the golden arch and a kindly Elf called Baelon, who took me on the last part of my journey to my new home and to meet my new friends. I have a nice comfy big bed and I'm allowed to eat anything I like, although Baelon did suggest last evening that perhaps seven shoshages was enough for my tea!

The first thing I noticed when I arrived, Mummy, is that I no longer felt ill, in fact I have the energy of a young Retriever again. Do you remember the long walks we used to go on together, Mummy? They are some of my best memories of our time together. Well a young Retriever called Olly took me to a field of tall golden barley on my first day and we spent many happy hours chasing each other through it. We then finished by swimming in the blue lake before one of the Elves dried us with thick, warm towels and fed us our tea. That's when I ate the seven shoshages!

And guess what, Mummy, there are two really tiny puppies here. I felt so sad when I saw them. They had to leave their mummies after only a few weeks. They have a new Mummy, called Maisie, who looks after them and she asked me if I wanted to play with them. Well, Mummy, it was wonderful. I lay on my back and they jumped on me and nibbled my ears, and they have squeaky little barks and yapped at me. Oh, Mummy, it was such great fun. We all look after them as they are so young, and my friend Olly says he can't wait to take them running through the Fields of Gold.

As I write this to you I'm sat on top of the hill that looks across the blue lake towards the arch where we all arrive.

It's the place we all come to when we want to be on our own and think of home. I'm still coming to terms with the sudden change in my life. It all happened so quickly, Mummy. I knew I was ill, and I could see how worried you were about me. But I also knew that you would always do the right thing by me. I knew that you loved me so much that when the time came you would do what was needed.

I fell asleep hearing you tell me that you loved me ...

I had the most wonderful life with you, Mummy. I was happiest when it was just you and me. The late evenings where you would cuddle me and talk to me, and the many hours we spent walking together. I want you to know I am happy here, Mummy. The Elves look after me and I have made some wonderful friends. Another young puppy arrived yesterday called Fudge. She looked lost just as I was when I first arrived, so I showed her around Rainbow Bridge. She seems to have taken to me so Olly and I will take her to play in the Fields of Gold later.

So, Mummy, I just wanted to make sure that you knew I was fine and that I've settled into my new home. I have all I need, the only thing missing for me is you. Olly has told me that If I want to dream of home that's the last thing I must think of before I fall asleep. And that's what I will be doing tonight.

Take care, my lovely Mummy, and be secure in the knowledge that I love you with every ounce of my being,

Your loving boy, Lennie.

*

Kevin's Journey

A Short Story by Ian O'Neill

Daetia the Unicorn was sad. Her job was to meet the dogs on their final journey and guide them to Rainbow Bridge. They were invariably lost and confused as they found their way through the mist and it was down to her to offer them friendship and solace. There was something natural when an old dog trod this path. The inevitability of life's journey would always lead them to Rainbow Bridge. But it was so different when puppies and young dogs made the same journey. Their lives had been cut short by fate's cruel hand and they would be very frightened when they arrived.

And today she waited for a young dog.

This young dog had fought the battle of his life to stay with his family, but sadly it wasn't to be. Daetia's heart ached for this young boy and she hoped that she could find the words of comfort that would help soothe him. She peered deep into the mist looking for him when something caught her eye. A dim light flickered in the distance. What is this, she thought?

She continued to stare into the swirling mist and other flickering lights slowly appeared one by one. They led from the human world and slowly made their way towards her. A thought struck her. This was a 'Guiding Light', a phenomenon she had heard of but had never seen before. This young dog's friends and family were guiding him on his journey with candles. The Unicorn thought her heart would sing with happiness. There was still such deep love in the human world despite so many troubles.

And then he appeared, trotting confidently beside the candles. A beautiful young Golden Retriever, his head held high and his fan tail erect and proud. He headed for Daetia and she was sure she saw a trace of a smile on his lips. He stopped in front of her, sat down and looked up at her with his beautiful dark brown eyes.

She smiled back down at him and said warmly, 'Welcome, Kevin. My name is Daetia, and I will take you on the next stage of your journey into Rainbow Bridge.' She leant down and nuzzled him, her tears falling onto his head and coat.

'Hello,' said Kevin tentatively, and nuzzled her back.

'My tears will help soothe your pain and fears, young Kevin.'

'My Mummy told me all about Rainbow Bridge,' said Kevin. 'She didn't want me to be frightened.'

'Your Mummy loves you very much, Kevin. No one could've done more to save you.'

'I have the best Mummy,' said Kevin. 'Together with my brother, Henry, we would have so much fun together. And when I was ill and at the vets she would come every day and talk to me. But I was so weak, Daetia. I did my best, but I just couldn't find the strength. But I feel lucky.'

Daetia looked confused. 'Why do you say you were lucky? Your life in the human world was ended much too soon.'

Kevin smiled enigmatically. 'My life may have been short, but it was full of fun and more love than any one Golden Retriever could ever need. We laughed, we played; oh Daetia, it was wonderful.'

The Unicorn was quickly realising that he was one very special young dog. 'Come Kevin, let us go through the golden arch. I have a friend you need to meet.'

They stepped through the arch side by side emerging onto the lush green grass of the meadow and were greeted by the kindly, smiling face of Baelon the Elf.

'Welcome young man. Welcome to Rainbow Bridge.'

Baelon knelt down and Kevin sat beside him. The Elf wrapped his arm around him and stroked his head. 'You will suffer no more pain, young Kevin. Your life from now will be full of love and play while you wait for your Mummy to come for you.'

Kevin looked up at Baelon, tears misted his eyes. 'I'm going to miss her so much.'

Baelon hugged him close. 'The pain you feel, Kevin, is a measure of the depth of your love for her. Your Mummy is a very special person. She loved you so much that she put an end to your suffering. An act of pure, selfless love, young Kevin.'

Kevin found some comfort in his words, but he would give anything to feel his Mummy's arms around him and her soft voice in his ear. But she'd always told him to be brave and that's what he was going to be.

'Come, young Kevin. Let me take you to your new home and meet your friends.'

Daetia leant over and kissed Kevin on his head. 'Take care, Kevin. I am always here watching over you.'

Kevin returned the kiss and stood alongside Baelon. 'I'm ready,' and off they trotted up the hill.

Kevin was greeted with the amazing spectacle of the flower covered stone bridge and the rainbow arc above it once he reached the top of the hill. He looked across the blue lake and up the far hill towards the Fields of Gold, before his attention was grabbed by several Goldies playing in front of a row of cottages.

'Your new friends,' said Baelon. 'They are all fine Goldens and will look after you, young Kevin.'

Kevin's fears slowly subsided as he watched them. It was typical Goldie play, lots of barking, running, rolling around – general mayhem. It was his type of fun.

As Baelon and Kevin approached the playing Goldies, one of them came bounding over. It was Olly. He stopped in front of Kevin and studied him for a moment.

'Welcome to Rainbow Bridge. My name is Olly.'

Kevin looked to Baelon for guidance and the Elf encouraged him to respond.

'I'm Kevin.'

Olly leant forward and nuzzled him in true Rainbow Bridge fashion. 'You are still only a puppy my young friend. I was barely twenty months old when I arrived here myself.' He turned to his friends who had now joined them. 'This is Bonnie, Zoe, Buddy, Doris and Kevin. Each one of them arrived here way too soon.' They each took turns in nuzzling Kevin. Just the contact made him feel so much more relaxed. And he had something very special in common with them.

'Come on guys, let's give Kevin a rousing Rainbow Bridge reception,' said Baelon.

'Olly and his pals didn't need any encouragement. They all sat in a row, threw their heads back and barked as loud as they could. Kevin looked on and a warm feeling built inside him. But then something special happened. More barking rang across from the other side of the lake and up in the hills. Barking came from every direction.

'That's Rainbow Bridge welcoming you, young Kevin. It's tradition for you to respond.'

Kevin couldn't remember the last time he had barked. He stood up, opened his mouth and let the most joyous bark rise from deep within him. His tail wagged in time and a rush of adrenaline streamed from the tip of his tail to the tip of his nose. He felt alive. He felt good.

Once the chorus came to a halt, Olly stepped forward. 'My friends and me are called the Pupstars. Would you like to join us? We play together and support each other as well as entertain the oldies!'

Kevin smiled for the first time since he arrived at the Bridge. 'I would love that.'

Olly ran around barking and frantically wagging his tail. 'Pawsome! We have another member guys.' The Pupstars barked their approval. 'Right,' continued Olly, 'now we must introduce you to the Fields of Gold. But first we must clear up your name.' He beckoned the other Kevin forward with his paw. He stepped forward and stood alongside Olly. Olly looked from one Kevin to the other.

'So, the new Kevin is bigger than our Kevin so will now be known as big Kevin, and you little fella, will be called little Kevin. Is that OK?'

Both Kevin's nodded their approval.

'Right then, Fields of Gold here we come. Are you ready Pupstars?'

The deafening barks told him they were. Baelon knelt down and whispered in big Kevin's ear. 'Go and enjoy yourself my young friend. I will see you later at supper time. Run free Kevin and embrace the magic of Rainbow Bridge.'

With that they all turned around and ran towards the hill that led to the Fields of Gold. Big Kevin ran by the side of Olly and felt wonderful. To feel the wind blowing around his ears and through his golden coat made him shudder with joy. And when they approached the field of tall golden barley, Olly sped off ahead of them shouting, 'Catch me if you can!' And the Pupstars chased after him barking with glee.

*

Kevin lay on top of the hill in front of the golden field gazing across the blue lake towards the golden arch on the far side of Rainbow Bridge. He had enjoyed a delicious meal of shoshages, mashed potatoes and thick tasty gravy. Olly had suggested that he may like some quiet time at the end of his first day at the Bridge. And he needed it. So much had happened to him over the last few days.

He'd made some wonderful friends and played games all afternoon. The Elves looked after their every need and there were Pixies to play with them any time they wanted for as long as they wanted. The surroundings were perfect, everything a Goldie could ever want or need. All that were missing were his Mummy and Henry. Oh how he missed them both.

Olly had told him about a hooman they called the Chronicler. They say he walks amongst them and writes about the dogs on Rainbow Bridge for their hooman families to read about. Everybody knows him but nobody knows him. Olly told him to say his words and not think them so that the Chronicler could record them. He took a deep breath and started.

'My wonderful Mummy, it is the end of my first day on Rainbow Bridge and I'm sitting on top of a hill looking towards the golden arch and longing for both you and Henry. I'm thinking about how much fun we all shared and the deep love that sustained us. Oh Mummy, when I was ill, just seeing you made me feel better, even when I was at my weakest. But I want you to know that I am happy and have already made some wonderful friends here. And guess what Mummy? I am one of Olly's Pupstars. We're a group of Goldies who all came here very young. We play together and look after each other and we entertain the older dogs! Already, we are great friends, Mummy.

Today we ran in the Fields of Gold and it was the most exhilarating feeling, Mummy. We chased Olly and no one has ever caught him until today. And guess who caught him, Mummy? Yes, it was me, your very own Kevin, or big Kevin as they call me here! The Elves are very kind to us and look after our every need, and the Pixies will play with us all day if we want. It really is a special place, or as Olly describes it, magical.

Another two older dogs arrived today, Ollie and Honey. They are both really friendly, Mummy, and they are running around like young dogs again. So, Ollie is right, Rainbow Bridge is a magical place.

Please think of me often, Mummy, as I will think of you and Henry. Baelon told me that love can never be parted and that we will always have that connection. I know that I was taken from you in the cruellest of circumstances but that could never break the bond that ties us. Our love is universal, Mummy, and will sustain us both until that time you come for me.

Tonight, before I go to sleep, Mummy, I will look out onto a full moon resting over Rainbow Bridge and my last thought before I go to sleep will be of you. Could I ask that you do the same and we will be together in our dreams. Always remember that this young Golden Retriever loves you with every ounce of his being. Please give Henry a big kiss on his nose from his little bro and tell him to make every day count. Tell him that I will never forget him and that I will always be waiting for him, but not to hurry.

Never forget me, Mummy, as I will never forget you.
Sending you the biggest, wettest kiss...
Your ever-loving little boy, Kevin.

*

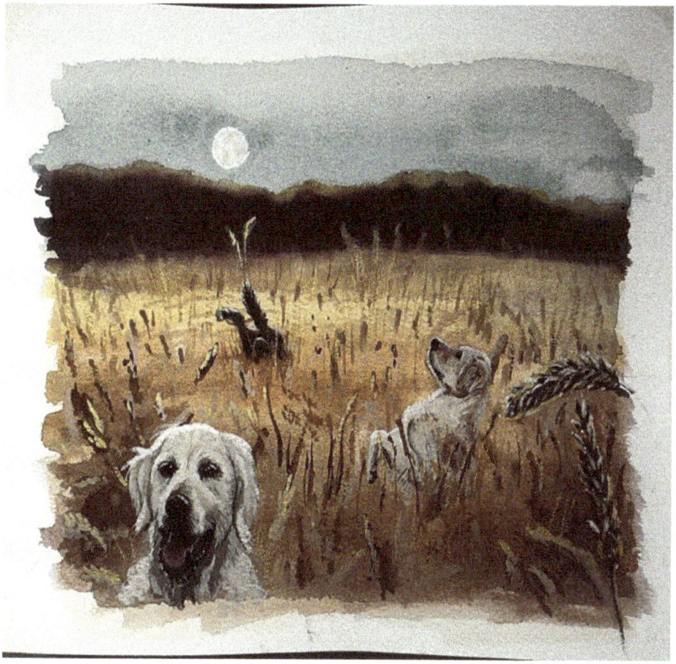

A Letter from Podge

A Short Story by Ian O'Neill

Podge lay at the top of the hill to the rear of the cottages. It was where the Goldens went to when they wanted time on their own. Podge was a social animal, he loved the company of his fellow Goldens, but today, he wanted time to reflect on his life. It was two years since he arrived at the Bridge and the longing for home was just that little bit stronger.

Not that he was unhappy because he had some wonderful friends on the Bridge. Harvey, Sonny, Rory, Bob, Jake, Maisie, Paddy, Charlie, Chip, and the young ones, Kevin, Zoe and Olly. He loved spending time with them; he loved their energy, and he loved their optimism. All doggie bowls were always half full for Olly.

In truth, they were all his friends, but this was a day for his own company. He took full advantage of the peace and solitude and composed a letter home: -

Dear Dad,

It's hard to believe that it's two years since I left you all. I think of home every day and long for the wonderful times we spent together. How I loved those long walks through the fields. Running in long grass and the golden corn; running through the woods and forests and sniffing all those wonderful smells. I never imagined that it would ever end. Those days were happy beyond belief.

I slowed down as I got older, but we still shared many hours together out in the fields. It's the place we loved the best, fresh air, space and water. Not that I ever jumped in any muddy puddles of course unlike my two younger bros! I do watch you in my dreams Dad and I love to see you smiling again. Ned and Finn bring you the joy you deserve. Would I like to run with you? You bet I would and join them in the deepest, muddiest puddles that we could find! And I smile when I hear your voice in my head. 'Oh Podge, I thought you would show these two rascals the clean puddles.'

I have a wonderful life on the Bridge. I have some amazing friends and every day is a feast of running in woods and fields and swimming in the clear blue lake by our cottages. I have taken to young Kevin, or more to the point, he's taken to me. He follows me, Harvey and Rory everywhere we go. Harvey says that we three are like the 'Last of the Summer Wine'! But I love the company of the young ones.

As happy as I am here, I miss the times we spent together, especially late at night when it was just the two of us. You would talk to me and sometimes share your troubles. You said I was the best listener that you'd ever known. And I was glad to do it as I was with you. I mean, where else would I want to be?

I had fifteen wonderful years with you, Mummy, and the girls. They were golden days, Dad, in more ways than one. How lucky was I to find you all? Of all the families I could've lived with I chose you. I was the luckiest dog alive. All I have to do is think back to those days and my heart sings again. But it aches a little too.

Dad, I want you to know that when you're missing me the most, that's the time when I'm missing you too. It's when our hearts cry out for each other. Baelon, the Elf, explained it to me. When the pain of separation is at its height, that's when we are the closest. Our memories entwine, our tears flow together, and the longing ... But that's when our love is at its strongest. The depth of that pain shows the true measure of our love, and it runs deep, my precious Dad.

So, as I sit here looking across the beautiful blue lake and the lush green meadows towards the arch, I send you my love. I think of the times you held me, and I think of the last time I smelt your scent and looked up into your kind eyes. Remember, I am never far from you, Dad, no more than a tear away.

Until that time when I see you walking towards me across that lush green meadow, take care, Dad, remembering you with so much love and affection, and yes, the longing. And give those two young rascals, Ned and Finn, a massive hug from their big bro.

Your special boy, your ever-loving Podge.

*

Murph's Diary

Loki's Story

A Short Story by Ian O'Neill

'When human dreams come together with animal dreams, that's where the magic happens.'

So, there I was having an evening stroll after me supper the other day when I saw a lone Golden sat on top of the hill by the Fields of Gold. He was looking across towards the golden arch. Nothing unusual in that, thought I, as many of us take ourselves up here when we're in need of a bit of solitude.

But as I walked past him he turned to me and said, 'Do you think I could go back home through the arch?'

He was only a young fella, and I couldn't help noticing the sad look on his face. And I'm sure I'd never seen him before.

'There isn't a dog on Rainbow Bridge who hasn't had the very same thought at some time or other. And some have even tried.'

'Did they get home?' he asked hopefully.

I shook my head. 'Sadly no. If you walk back through the arch it doesn't take you anywhere other than Rainbow Bridge. Unless you're a Unicorn of course.'

The young fella turned back towards the arch. Me aul heart ached for seeing him so sad. 'You haven't been here long, have you young fella? What's your name?'

'Loki. I've been here a few days.'

'That's a grand name.'

'I'm not really sure what happened,' said Loki. 'I've been ill for a long time. I was at home with my Mummy and Daddy and my brother, Cooper, when I went to sleep. The next thing I knew I was walking through a mist and could hear someone calling my name. It was Daetia the Unicorn, and she took me through the arch to Rainbow Bridge where I met Baelon. He brought me to the cottages and my brother, Rolo, and sister, Tally, were waiting for me.' I saw the tears in the young fella's eyes. 'They've been looking after me. I have a bed in between theirs.'

'It's the journey we all take. It's grand your brother and sister met you. I've run many times with the both of them. And I'm guessing you met Olly when you arrived.'

Loki smiled for the first time. 'Yes, he took me for a run in the Fields of Gold. I really liked that.'

'Young or old, everyone gets introduced to the Fields when they arrive,' I said smiling.

'Do you think I will ever go home again?' said Loki.

I sat down by his side and rested me paw on his shoulder. 'Of course you will, but not in the way you think. I often dream of home and I'm sure I'm actually there. I see me Mammy and Daddy, and Luce and Henry, even me new sister, Rosy. And I always wake with a wonderful warm feeling.'

'I hope I dream of home too,' said Loki.

'I'm sure you will.' A flicker of a smile crossed his lips. It was grand to see. 'Where are you from young fella?'

'Somerset. I loved it there. My Mummy and Daddy used to take me for walks in the hills with my brother Cooper. They were such happy times.'

Now it was my turn to feel homesick. 'Jeez, I loved those Somerset hills too, although me favourite was the beaches. I spent many happy hours running through the sea.'

'I loved the beaches too. We lived right by one. Me and Cooper would chase each other along the sand and through the sea.'

'And those golden memories will stay with us forever, Loki. And you can be sure that your Mammy and Daddy will remember those precious times too. And Cooper of course.'

He sat quietly lost in his own thoughts for a few moments. 'It's just that I feel so lonely. I miss Cooper so much.'

'I felt the same when I arrived. Don't get me wrong, I love me two older bros, Sonny and Rory, but I really miss Luce and Henry. The three of us had some right aul battles. There was never a quiet moment with them two around.'

'I love Tally and Rolo too, they have been so kind to me since I arrived. But …'

'They're not Cooper,' said I.

Loki nodded his head.

'You will make lots of friends here, Loki. Just remember that all of the dogs here felt exactly the same as you do now when they first arrived. Why do you think Olly takes all new arrivals to the Fields of Gold?'

Loki shook his head. 'I don't know.'

'Because he wants to show them something that's familiar to them. Show me a dog who doesn't love to run through a field of tall barley? We all strive to make it as normal as possible while we wait for our Mammies and Daddies together. And talking of Mammies and Daddies, there's our Maisie. She's the Mammy of us all on Rainbow Bridge. She's a great listener and has words of wisdom for every occasion. I'll introduce you when we go back to our cottages.'

Murphy leant into Loki and gave him a snuggle. 'You'll be fine, young fella, I promise.'

'Will you be my friend, Murphy?' asked Loki.

'I'd be proud to. You can be one of the Likely Lads with me and me mate Paddy B. Mind you, according to Olly, me and the other Likely Lads are the old fogies.'

'I don't mind being with the old fogies,' said Loki smiling.

'And we'll love having you with us. Our runs are much more sedate affairs than the Pupstars but just as much fun.'

'Will my Mummy and Daddy know I'm safe?' asked Loki.

'That's where the magic comes into play,' said I. 'There's a mystery hooman who walks the hallowed turf of Rainbow Bridge. He's known as the Chronicler. Everybody knows him but nobody knows him. He passes messages to our hoomans back home.'

'Do you think he knows about our conversation?'

'I think he just might,' I smiled. 'Why don't you send a message now to your Mammy and Daddy.'

The young fella turned towards the arch. He sat quietly for a few moments, and then delivered his message for home.

'Mummy and Daddy, I just wanted you to know that I arrived safely on Rainbow Bridge. Tally and Rolo came to meet me. I like having my brother and sister with me. I sleep in between them every night. I feel like a young dog again and I run through a field of tall barley every day. Rolo says that it's the magic of Rainbow Bridge that is healing me.

I have a new friend. His name is Murphy. He comes from Somerset too. He says that there is a hooman called the Chronicler who takes messages home from the dogs on Rainbow Bridge, so I hope you get this.

I had the five most wonderful years with you. I so wish it could've been longer, but it wasn't to be. Murphy tells me I can come home in my dreams, so look out for me, Mummy and Daddy, I will be there with you when you're missing me the most. Give Cooper a big snuggle from me and tell him I miss him. And I hope the Chronicler will bring more messages from me, so you know what I'm up to. I will think of you all every day, as I hope you will think of me.

I will hold onto the happy memories we made together. They were the best of times, and they will stay with me forever. Even though I was ill you made my last few months special. We did all the things I loved most together, and they are held firmly within my heart. The pain of leaving you is still raw at the moment, but Rolo assured me that it lessens over time and one day I will be able to smile again.

Please don't worry about me. I know I will be looked after here, and Murphy assures me I will make lots of new friends. The Elves are very kind, and the Pixies play with us whenever we want. I had shoshages for supper last night and they were pawsome. That's a word Olly made up by the way and I like using it. Olly is even younger than me. He wasn't even two when he came here. I think it's so sad that young dogs have to leave their Mummies and Daddies.

Every night, before I go to sleep I think of you all at home. It makes me feel closer to you all. I will say goodbye for now and will tell Tally and Rolo that I have sent you a message.

Sending you all my love, and a special snuggle for Izzy and Cooper,

Your ever-loving Golden boy, Loki.'

Well, I stood by him, the tears streaming down me face. I snuggled the young fella again and said, 'Time for us to head back to the cottages, Loki me lad. We don't want to miss out on the bedtime biccies now do we?'

We exchanged smiles and the two of us trotted off back down the hill happily chatting away to one another.

"To live in hearts we leave behind is not to die." – Thomas Campbell

Wonka and Mungo

A Short Story by Ian O'Neill

Wonka and Mungo stood alongside Baelon the Elf, the Guardian of Rainbow Bridge. The flower covered stone steps above them reached up to and beyond the heavenly blue sky. A beautiful, brightly coloured rainbow straddled the bridge.

Baelon knelt down in between them and placed his arms around their shoulders. 'Rainbow Bridge my friends. You have arrived safely.'

The two dogs looked nervously around. In the time since they'd left home they'd travelled through the mist and were welcomed by a beautiful Unicorn. She guided them through a golden arch onto the lush green grass. And now they stood with an Elf under the magnificent stone steps.

It was a lot for them to take in. So much had happened to them in a short span of time. Only a matter of hours before they had had to say a tearful goodbye to their Mummy, Daddy, Ben, Toby, Kate, and Jack, the black Labrador, their younger brother.

'Is this our new home?' asked Wonka.

'It is indeed,' said a smiling Baelon. 'It is a place where there is no illness, no pains and no worries. You will have everything you need, my young friends.'

Wonka and Mungo exchanged nervous looks.

'But we don't know anyone here,' said Mungo. 'We have no friends to play with.'

'Every dog on Rainbow Bridge is your friend. They all look after each other here.' Baelon stood up. 'Come, let me introduce you to them.'

The three of them walked slowly down the hill towards a row of cottages to the side of the blue lake. As they neared the cottages two dogs approached. One, a Golden Retriever, the other a Chocolate Labrador just like themselves. Wonka and Mungo exchanged knowing looks.

'Jackson? Wembley? Is that really you?'

Jackson and Wembley both had broad smiles as they happily trotted up to them.

'Welcome to Rainbow Bridge,' said Jackson.

He and Wembley snuggled Wonka and Mungo, the traditional Rainbow Bridge welcome for new arrivals.

Just seeing their old friends again made Wonka and Mungo relax a little.

'Would you like to run with us through the Fields of Gold?' asked Wembley.

Wonka and Mungo looked to Baelon.

'Go, my young friends, and enjoy yourselves. I will see you both later at supper time.'

Wonka and Mungo followed Jackson and Wembley past the cottages and up the hill to the side. As they approached the brow of the hill, they saw a field of golden barley stretched out before them. A young Golden Retriever suddenly appeared out of the barley. His face wore a huge smile and his tail wagged excitedly. When he saw the four of them he came bounding over.

'And who is it we have here, Jackson?' he asked.

'Olly, this is Wonka and Mungo. They have just arrived at Rainbow Bridge.'

'What pawsome names,' said Olly. 'Do you like to run through golden fields?'

'It's been a while,' said Mungo.

'Well, it's about time you did it again,' smiled Olly. 'The magic of Rainbow Bridge will cure those aching old bones.'

They both stretched their legs.

'They don't hurt anymore,' said Wonka.

'Nor mine,' said Mungo his tail wagging excitedly.

'Well,' said Olly bouncing up and down on the spot, 'in that case, it's about time you chased me through the fields. Catch me if you can!' And he ran headlong into the tall barley.

'After you,' said Wembley gesturing towards the barley.

With that, the four friends ran headlong into the tall barley and disappeared.

*

It was some hours later when they all emerged from the barley and flopped down onto the lush green grass.

'So, boys, did you have fun?' asked Olly.

'It was pawsome!' panted Wonka.

'Yes it was,' said Mungo in between breaths.

Jackson and Wembley were also panting heavily. 'I haven't run that far since the last time,' laughed Jackson.

There was a question that was bothering Wonka. 'I was wondering … I was wondering where Mungo and I are going to sleep tonight?'

'In the beds next to me and Wembley of course. They are already in place,' said Jackson.

'But how did you know we were coming?' asked Mungo.

'The Chronicler told Baelon,' said Jackson.

'Who is the Chronicler?' asked Wonka.

'He's a hooman who writes about us all,' said Olly. 'He walks the hallowed turf of Rainbow Bridge. Everybody knows him, but nobody knows him. I wouldn't be at all surprised if he's writing about this.'

'Really,' said Wonka. 'Do you think he would tell our family at home that we have arrived safely and not to worry about us?'

'I'm sure he would,' said Jackson.

Wonka and Mungo turned towards the golden arch in the distance. Tears misted their eyes as they thought of home.

Wonka spoke for them both. 'Mummy, Daddy, Ben, Toby, Kate, Jack, we are here on Rainbow Bridge. Jackson and Wembley met us, and we have been playing with them and our new friend Olly in the Fields of Gold. And Jack, would you believe that Mungo and I can run like young dogs again? We could really give you a good run! It is really beautiful here and everyone has been so kind, so please don't worry about us.' He hesitated for a moment and rested his paw on his brother's shoulder. 'We shared so many happy times with you all and loved being part of your family. Think of us both often as we will think of you. And remember, we are waiting … always waiting.'

Jackson and Wembley stood either side of them and snuggled them both.

'Come up here when you're missing home. Every time you talk to them they will see a rainbow. Or a robin will settle near them. Or perhaps a feather will drop at their feet. I can assure you both that they will never forget you,' said Jackson.

In the distance they hear the sound of a gong.

'Supper time,' said Olly. 'Shoshages and gravy tonight.'

'I love shoshages,' said Mungo.

'Name me a dog who doesn't,' laughed Olly. 'I'll race you back to the cottages.'

With that, the five of them sprang onto their paws and raced each other down the hill.

*

A Letter Home
(Brothers in Paws)

A Short Story by Ian O'Neill

These mist covered green hills,
Are home now for me,
But my home was the mid lands,
And always will be,
My heart will return to,
With courage and noble cause,
And I will forever yearn to be,
With my brothers in paws ...

Dear Mummy,

I wanted you to know that I've arrived safely on Rainbow Bridge. I was accompanied on the last leg of my journey by a kindly Elf called Baelon. It was as I walked by his side up a grassy hill towards my new home that I saw them. Three dogs sat upon the brow of the hill were silhouetted against the full moon. My nose twitched at the familiar scents, and I intuitively knew they were my brothers.

Well, Olly came bounding up to me and we had an amazing snuggle. He was followed by Toby. I felt quite emotional meeting him and we both shed tears of joy at seeing each other again. And then I was introduced to our eldest brother, Max. He was calm and assuring and gave me a gentle snuggle. Oh Mummy, I can't begin to describe the feelings coursing through me at that moment. My sadness at leaving you all was tempered by the joy of being with my brothers.

I was taken to meet all the other Golden Retrievers who were waiting by the cottages. It was overwhelming but wonderful too. And guess what, Mummy? There are Fields of Gold here just like at home. Olly runs through them every day with his Pupstars. So early the next morning, after breakfast, the four brothers headed up the hill towards the Fields of Gold.

I felt like a young dog again running and barking through the golden barley. And Olly told me that it stays the same all year round. I'm fast realising that Rainbow Bridge is full of magic. My nose has healed, and all my aches and pains have gone. And I can run all day and even keep up with Olly!

I have a lovely bed alongside Max, Toby and Olly. The four Callicott boys sleep together, eat together, and play together. Except sometimes when Olly wants to spend his day running with his Pupstars, and that's when Max, Toby and me discreetly return to the cottage and rest up with some of the other Goldens.

Every day is a journey of discovery. We run through lush green meadows. We run up and down rolling hills. We splash in streams that are as pure as the mountain dew. And, of course, the muddy ponds covered in green slime are our favourite, although the Elves are not so amused when we troop back to the cottages covered in mud and slime! But a quick swim in the crystal blue lake and we're golden again.

I'm sitting on top of the hill by the Fields of Gold and staring across towards the golden arch I stepped through just a few days ago. It is the place all the dogs come to when they want some quiet time. Olly suggested I come up here and gather my thoughts. He said there is a hooman who walks the hallowed turf of Rainbow Bridge. He carries messages from the dogs to their families back home.

So, I hope these thoughts find their way to you, Mummy, as I want you to know I am well, and happy to be with my brothers. I have met so many dogs since I've been here that it's hard to remember all the names. I am one of the Likely Lads, along with Max and Toby. There are a few of us who run together when we explore the hidden treasures of Rainbow Bridge. Olly says that we're the old fogies, but we don't mind. Murphy O says that Olly is a cheeky little fecker which makes us all laugh.

I have been lucky in my life that I was part of a loving and kind family. And that made it harder for me leaving you and coming to Rainbow Bridge. But I've experienced so much kindness since I arrived. Not just from the other dogs but the Elves and Pixies too. They do everything they can to make us feel loved and secure. And the magic ensures that we stay healthy. I feel like a young dog again, bursting with vitality and energy. And I can assure you I need it with Olly around!

So, Mummy, I just wanted you to know I was safe and well. I want to thank you for thirteen wonderful years with the most loving family a dog could ever wish for. Give Bennie and Raffi a hug from their older brother, and little Scrappy too. When the brothers are together we often talk about home. We remember the wonderful times we spent with you, Daddy, Vicky and Cat – Our hooman family. They are wonderful and precious memories, Mummy, and will stay with us boys forever.

Take care, Mummy, and think of me often. And don't feel sad as I am happy and safe within the loving embrace of my three brothers, the Callicott boys … my brothers in paws.

Your ever-loving Golden boy, Bailey.

*

Lottie's Tale

A Short Story by Ian O'Neill

I lost a special friend today
The kind you can't replace
And looking at her empty bed
I still see her beautiful face
I know she's in a special place
Where dogs can play all day
Lush meadows fields and flowers
Help make them strong and whole again
I know she's watching over me
She'll be with me when I cry
So, with one more kiss on her beloved head
I told my friend goodbye ...
                                              Anon.

Hello,

My name is Lottie and I'm a Golden Retriever. I'm sitting on top of the hill where all of us Goldens come to when we need some quiet time. It's next to the Fields of Gold where we all chase Olly. I love Olly. We all love Olly. He plays all the time. His big brother Max says if there were twenty-five hours in a day that Olly would play for every one of them!

I live on Rainbow Bridge now. I've been here for over a week. But I used to live with my Mummy and Daddy. And Fia, and William and Molly and Rowan (everyone calls him Roo). They were my hooman family. I love my hooman family. I had the most wonderful life with them. I was just a puppy when I found them. And Fia, William and Roo were just puppies too. Oh, we had so much fun. I chased them around the garden. They would laugh, and I would bark. My tail wagged like a windmill. They were good times. Times

I will never forget.

I like chasing balls. My favourite are tennis balls. I spent most of my life chasing tennis balls. Even when I was old and achy I still loved to hold a tennis ball in my mouth. The Pixies will throw tennis balls for us all day. I love the Pixies. They will play with us for as long as we want. I chased a tennis ball into the pond last week and came out covered in mud and green slime. Well, when Shana the Elf saw me she laughed and said, 'Oh Lottie, how am I going to get you clean again?' Well, it was easy. She took me to the clear blue lake under the stone steps and threw a tennis ball right into the middle of it. I jumped in the lake and swam out to the ball and brought it back to her. After the tenth time I was clean. Easy.

I love shoshages. I had shoshages for tea last night. Podge is the shoshage monster according to Olly. I used to watch my Daddy eating shoshages. He likes them too. Sometimes he'd give me one. My Daddy taught me a trick. He would place a biscuit on my nose, and I had to balance it until he gave me the command. And when he did I would flip it up in the air and catch it in my mouth. And then he did it with two biscuits and then three. I showed my new friends the trick last night. Olly said I was pawsome! He makes me laugh.

The last few years with my hooman family were special. I was getting old. My legs ached, and my back ached. My hearing wasn't good, and my eyesight was poor. But I still wanted to play. Someone called me the forever puppy. I think that's about right. Life is for playing. I loved running on beaches. I used to chase the ball into the sea and swim out to collect it. Then I'd bring it back for my hoomans to throw again. Life is simple and uncomplicated when you're a Golden Retriever. Eat, play and sleep.

My last weeks were difficult. I could no longer walk very far. My Mummy did everything she could to help me. I had a lady who put pins in me. And another lady who massaged me. I liked the massage better than the pins. I felt so precious that I had the best of everything. But the best thing

I had was my hooman family. They made me the richest Golden Retriever in the world.

And I knew my time was coming. My family tended to my every need. But I looked at my Mummy and Daddy one morning and they cried, because they knew too. They took me out into the sun and let me have one last lay in my garden. I lay with my hooman family. William, Molly and Roo stroked me and whispered words to me that I will never forget.

My Daddy carried me back into the house and I lay with the people who I loved. My Mummy cooked me fish. It was delicious; and then ice cream. And then the stranger came. I lay with my family and ate chocolate, and drifted off into a peaceful sleep, bathed by the loving tears of my family.

My journey continued. I met a Unicorn, then an Elf. I arrived on Rainbow Bridge. Well not on, under. The flower covered stone steps reached to the sky, a rainbow arc to its side. I stood alongside Baelon the Elf marvelling at the beauty. I looked down towards the cottages that were to be my new home. Golden Retrievers played on the lush green grass and swam in the blue lake beneath the steps.

Then it struck me. My body no longer ached, and I could hear and see. I felt like a young dog once again. Baelon told me that it was the healing magic of Rainbow Bridge. As I approached the cottages, all the dogs stopped playing and turned towards me. And then as one they began barking. The barks resonated all around me. The whole of Rainbow Bridge was welcoming me. I looked to Baelon, and he encouraged me to respond. I threw my head back and barked as loud as I could, and it felt wonderful.

I have so many new friends. We play every day. I love to chase the ball into the lake. I'll happily do this all day. Sometimes I chase Olly and the Pupstars in the Fields of Gold. There are some really young dogs here. Cody, Bambi and Little Sausage were only puppies when they arrived here. That makes me feel sad. I had over fourteen wonderful years with my hooman family and they only had weeks with theirs.

So much has happened to me in such a short time. I've barely had time to think until now. I'm looking towards the golden arch and wondering about home. As happy as I am here I'm missing the closeness of my family. Sonny and Rory have been here a long time and told me that sometimes you feel like that and that it's only natural. They said that we leave our hooman family to go to a Golden one. Our Golden family isn't a replacement for our hooman family but one that we can share our sad times with and the good times too.

They also told me about the mysterious hooman that walks among us. They call him the Chronicler. Everybody knows him, but nobody knows him. I'm not sure what that means but he tells the hooman world stories from Rainbow Bridge. I like that. I want my hooman family to remember me as I will remember them.

Mummy, Daddy, Fia, William, Molly, Rowan, how blessed was I to have you as my family? You may think that you chose me all those years ago, but the truth is I chose you. As soon as I saw you I knew that you were the family for me. My earliest memories are of playing in the garden with Fia, William and Rowan. I remember the laughter. I remember being happy. I remember Christmas. I remember Santa Paws. I remember presents and all the paper strewn over the floor. They were truly golden times for us all.

I have been lucky to share my life with you all. I have been loved, truly loved and in return I loved you all, and always will. Love is music to the soul and my heart sings for you. Never stop talking to me as I will still hear you. Whisper those words and let the soft breeze carry them to me …

Mummy, you did everything possible to make my life comfortable over the latter years. I rarely felt any pain and it was only the last weeks where it got too much … and you knew that. The many times you whispered to me and I was happy just as long as you were holding me close. We shared many moments, Mummy, moments that I will always treasure. Don't be sad when you think of me. Think of your

Lottie following you everywhere, tail wagging. Think of me chasing a tennis ball. Think of me swimming. Think of me playing. Always think of me …

Your forever loving Golden girl, Lottie.

*

Buddy

A Short Story by Ian O'Neill

Buddy walked alongside Baelon the Elf as they slowly climbed the hill that would take him to his new home. So much had happened to him in such a short time. He was at home when he lay down and fell asleep. It was to be his final sleep and he left behind his Mammy who loved him dearly and his brother Charlie, and his sisters Angel and Sadie. And like all new arrivals on Rainbow Bridge he was feeling bewildered.

He'd walked through the mist and found Daetia the Unicorn. She took him through the golden arch to meet Baelon, the Guardian of the Bridge. They explained to him that he was on the next stage of his life journey, and he would wait here until it was his Mammy's time to join him.

It was as they neared the brow of the hill that two Goldens approached them. Baelon smiled broadly and gave them his usual warm welcome. 'Murphy, Paddy, meet your new friend. This is Buddy.'

Both Murphy and Paddy gave him the traditional Rainbow Bridge snuggle before stepping back.

'Welcome Buddy, it's grand to see you. Especially so as you're an IRR dog,' said Murphy.

'You know about IRR,' said Buddy.

'Yes we do,' said Paddy. 'Both Murphy and I were rescued by them many years ago. We owe them for giving us the wonderful lives we both had.'

'And so we wanted to meet you and show you around Rainbow Bridge and make sure you feel at home. Is it OK if we take him from here, Baelon?' said Murphy.

Baelon looked to Buddy. 'Are you OK with that? Or I can take you to the cottages if you prefer.'

Buddy seemed a little uncertain. Both Murphy and Paddy stood tails wagging in anticipation.

'Please say yes,' said Murphy. 'You'll have a grand aul

time with us.'

'I'm not sure I can run very far,' said Buddy.

'I bet you can,' said Paddy. 'Have a stretch and see how you feel.'

Buddy did just that, stretching out his front and back legs. 'I don't have any aches and pains,' he said as his tail started to wag for the first time since he arrived.

'That's the magic of Rainbow Bridge healing you,' said Baelon. 'Go with the boys, young Buddy, and enjoy yourself. I'll see you later at the cottages when it's time for supper.'

'Let's go,' said Murph, and the three of them ran to the brow of the hill.

Buddy stopped and looked up in awe at the flower covered stone steps that stretched high into the sky. But it was the rainbow that straddled it that really caught his attention. 'So there really is a Rainbow Bridge.'

'It's wonderful isn't it,' said Paddy. 'One day, when your Mummy arrives you'll climb those steps together.'

'But not for a while,' said Murphy. 'Come, let's run.'

And off they sped, running through the meadow and beyond. Buddy was amazed at just how well he felt. He stretched his legs out just as he did as a young dog. Sometimes he ran alongside Murphy and Paddy, sometimes in front, and sometimes behind. It was wonderful to feel the wind in his face again. Running was freedom and Buddy was squeezing every last ounce of joy from his first run in a long time.

They ran through green fields, up hills, down hills, through forests and splashed in shallow streams. It was exhilarating to do and to watch. They eventually stopped on the top of a hill at the heart of Rainbow Bridge. All three of them flopped onto the grass and lay there, pink tongues hanging out, panting.

'So, Buddy lad,' said Murphy in between breaths, 'did you enjoy that?'

'It was amazing. I'd forgotten how much I loved to just run.'

'We run every day,' said Paddy. 'There's always plenty of dogs who will happily join you.'

The three lads lay for a while as they caught their breaths. They then sat up and scanned around the lush fields of Rainbow Bridge. Murphy spotted some dogs playing in a stream in the distance.

'Shall we join those dogs playing over there? We can introduce you.'

Paddy looked at Murphy and winked. Buddy didn't seem sure.

'Can we run again, just the three of us?'

'Why don't we run across and say a quick hello and then we can go on our way,' suggested Murphy.

'Come Buddy, it will be fun,' said Paddy.

So the three lads set off once again and ran down the hill towards where the dogs were playing. Buddy hung back and both Paddy and Murphy sensed his apprehension. As they approached the dogs they slowed down to a trot and headed over to them. When they were just a few metres away one of the dogs came over.

'Hi Paddy, hi Murph. Have you come for a splash?' asked Laurel.

Buddy sat back and watched them. When Laurel spotted him his mouth opened wide and his jaw dropped.

'Buddy? 'Is that you?'

Buddy looked up and his body language instantly changed. 'Laurel?' Both their tails suddenly rose and wagged in unison. Their noses twitched as they recognised each other.

Laurel suddenly bounded forward and snuggled Buddy in true Rainbow Bridge fashion. 'Oh bro it's so good to see you.' He turned to the other dogs playing in the stream. 'Look who it is.'

The mayhem suddenly stopped as they all looked over. Then once they recognised Buddy they came bounding across and mobbed their brother. There was much joy with barking and leaping around.

'Buddy is that really you?' said Hardy, his tail wagging

so fast that he was in danger of taking off!

Then Cooper, Joy and Gromit joined in the welcome. Murphy and Paddy took a discreet step back as they watched the family reunion. There were three dogs who stood back and watched. Laurel called them over.

'Ragsy, Poochie, Sheila, this is your little bro, Buddy.'

They trotted over and made their welcomes albeit a little less energetically than their siblings. Then Laurel turned his attention to Paddy and Murphy.

'How did you know Buddy was our brother?'

'Baelon told us. He came looking for you as he was going to collect Buddy,' said Murphy. 'We knew you'd gone out for the day, so we offered to go with him and meet your bro. Then we took him for a run and ended up on top of Rainbow Hill. We knew we'd see where you were from there and that's when we brought him down to you.'

'Thanks lads,' said Hardy.' You two are the best.'

'That's what we do on Rainbow Bridge,' said Paddy. 'We look out for each other. Especially the IRR boys and girls.'

'You'll have a lot of catching up to do,' said Murphy, 'so we'll head off. And don't be late for supper.' With that they ran off across the meadow.

The dogs all shook vigorously to rid themselves of any excess water and then lay down on the grass.

'So, little bro, what happened?' asked Laurel.

'I'm not sure,' said Buddy. 'I lay down and went into a deep sleep. When I woke I was walking through a mist. Then I met Daetia.'

'Our poor Mammy,' said Joy, 'she must be heartbroken.'

'She will be indeed,' said Laurel sadly.

'I'm glad that Charlie, Angel and Sadie are there to take care of her,' said Buddy.

'Our Mammy is the best,' said Gromit. 'She was so gentle with me when I came to her house. I was in a bad way, and she nursed me back to health. Bit by bit my confidence grew. I wasn't sure I could trust a hooman ever again but her patience with me was endless. She wrapped me in a blanket of love and kindness. And I fell in love with her. I was heartbroken when I left her.'

'I don't remember much of my old life,' said Hardy. 'Probably because I don't want to. Our Mammy showed us all what a loving family could be, and we all love her for that.'

'We do indeed,' said Laurel.

'Baelon says that the carers like our Mammy are the best of the best and they are accorded a special welcome when they arrive on Rainbow Bridge,' said Joy.

'And our Mammy would rightly deserve such a welcome,' said Hardy, 'but not for a good while yet.'

They all nodded their agreement.

'Can I ask a question?' said Buddy coyly.

'You can ask anything,' said Laurel.

'Where will I sleep tonight?'

'You will sleep with your brothers and sisters in our cottage,' said Laurel. 'It has a wonderful open fire with comfortable beds. You will be warm and safely held within the loving care of your family.'

Buddy felt safe for the first time since he'd arrived on Rainbow Bridge. The shock of leaving his Mammy was still raw but he was with his brothers and sisters, and he knew she would be reassured by that. But there was something else that was bothering him.

'How will Mammy know that I arrived on Rainbow Bridge safely and that I'm with you all?'

'She'll know,' said Laurel. 'And there's a hooman called the Chronicler who walks the hallowed turf of Rainbow Bridge. He writes stories about the dogs here. I'm sure he'll get to hear about you arriving and will write your story.'

Buddy felt reassured but still felt an overwhelming sadness at leaving his Mammy. His brothers and sisters sensed it. They had all walked the same path and understood how he was feeling.

'You're hurting at the moment, Buddy,' said Joy, 'and it always will, but it lessens over time. All of us can reassure you that our Mammy's love will stay with you. We may be separated from her, but she lives strong in our hearts. There isn't a day goes by where we don't talk about her and reminisce about the happy times we shared.'

'And there are the dreams,' said Gromit. 'My dreams of home are vivid, and I could swear I'm with Mammy in her bedroom watching her sleep.'

Hardy placed a reassuring paw on his brother's shoulder. 'Little bro, we're all here for you. We're a family and always will be.'

Buddy forced a smile. He was feeling sad, but it was understandable. And there was another pressing issue for him.

'Can I ask another question?'

'You can ask anything little bro,' said Hardy.

'What times supper because I'm starving.'

His brothers and sisters all burst out laughing.

'You're a typical Golden,' laughed Laurel. 'We'll head back to the cottages. Shoshages for supper tonight.'

They all stood up and had another shake and they trotted off together, happily chatting and surrounding their little brother with their love and companionship.

*

The Hardest Goodbye

A Poem by Marisa Piedade

For you
My heart is breaking
For you
My soul is aching
Where are you hiding?
They took you away
They took you forever
And I have to stay
When I close my eyes
I feel you here
Sweet memories
No more pain or fear
Come back Golden angel
Let's go for a walk
I could tell you everything
Without even talk
Just cross the bridge
Find your way home
Without you I am lost
I feel so alone
I know it is all over
So I cry once again
I've lost more than a pet
I lost my best friend
Such great love
Can't just disappear
I can feel your presence
I know you are here
You will look over me
And my family too
Until the day
I cross over with you

Perfection

A Poem by Maria Piedade

God looked down
Saw that girl alone
So HE gave her a dog
To turn her house into a home
God made him gentle
With a Golden heart
HE made him loyal
So they'd never be apart
God made him calm
To cuddle in bed
HE made him also playful
To never let her be sad
God gave him a tongue
To lick away all her tears
And HE made him big
To scare away all her fears
God smiled and was happy
With what HE had done
But he had so much perfection
That he could not last long
That's why I treasure every day
With my lovely fur family
Although I love them so much
They can't be forever with me
I collect Golden memories
Every day in my heart
So I can have them forever
When we finally have to be apart!

One of a Kind

A Poem by Marisa Piedade

You are not rare
But you are one of a kind
If they can't see it
They are out of their mind
I don't care if you're rescued
Or if you have a pedigree
I took you to my home
And you are family to me
I don't care what's your colour
If you're cream or you're gold
I don't care your age
If you're young or you're old
With those little paws
You stole my heart
And only death
Will tear us apart.

A Letter from Louis

A Short Story by Ian O'Neill

Dear Mummy,

Thank you for choosing me to be your special boy. How lucky was I to have the best Mummy in the world? I don't remember much about my life before I met you, probably because I don't want to. But every moment with you has been wonderful. You have given me everything you could and more, and for that, I will always love you. We shared some happy times, some sad ones too. Oh Mummy, I hated seeing you unhappy and I always did my best to make sure you knew how much I loved you.

Although our time together was short, we made the best of every minute. You did everything to make me comfortable and pain free. I'd never met anyone so kind until you invited me into your life. I can't begin to tell you how happy that made me. I knew I loved you and wanted you to be my Mummy the moment I met you. I was the luckiest Golden Retriever in the world, all the bad memories and the hurt and the pain evaporated when you became my Mummy.

And now I'm at Rainbow Bridge. It is a magical place. There are green meadows, forests, lakes and a field full of golden barley where we run. And yes, Mummy, I can run now. The magic has taken all my pain away and I am like a young dog again. Please don't worry about me, Mummy, as I am happy here. I have met some wonderful friends and the Elves look after us all. It truly is a beautiful place. I have everything I need ... that is, except you, my darling Mummy. I'm going to miss our cuddles at night when you would hold me if I was in pain, and the whispered words of comfort that sustained me through it all.

When you're missing me the most, that is when I will be missing you. You must think of me, and I will think of you.

Then whisper those words and let the breeze carry them to me. I will never forget you; I will never forget how you showed me what it was to be loved, truly loved. It was a precious gift, Mummy, that no money or all the gold in the world could buy.

Please give Lottie a big hug from her brother, and promise me Mummy, that when you're ready, you will bring another rescue dog into your house and show them how wonderful it is to be loved. You are special, Mummy, you need to remember that.

I will never forget you; until we are together again, sending you all my love for now and forever...

Your special Golden boy, Louis.

*

The Golden Girls

A Short Story by Ian O'Neill

A Golden Retriever suddenly rushed out of the tall barley and threw herself onto the grass. Three more followed in quick succession and they also threw themselves onto the grass next to her. They lay there panting with their long pink tongues hanging out the side of their mouths.

'Where does Olly get his energy?' panted Lottie.

'I wish I knew,' said Meg in between breaths.

'Let me know if you find out,' gasped Jasmyne, 'as I could do with some.'

'Now I like a run as much as the next Golden,' said Paris catching her breath, 'but Olly and his Pupstars are too much for me.'

'They'll be in there for hours,' said Meg, 'and I bet they haven't even noticed we've gone yet.'

'I'd bet my last Bonio on it,' said Lottie.

'That's one of Murphy O's expressions,' smiled Jasmyne.

'Murph has an expression for everything,' said Lottie.

'I think our Lottie has a bit of a soft spot for Murph,' said Paris winking at her sister.

'He makes me smile,' said Lottie, 'and he's always so happy.'

'I love the Likely Lads,' said Meg. 'They're all very funny and very handsome.'

'Brody is a fine-looking Golden for sure,' said Jasmyne, 'and he's very charming. He calls me Princess Jas.'

'I think our Brody has an eye for a pretty girl,' said Paris. 'I'll have to keep an eye on my little sister.'

Lottie sat up and looked across the blue lake towards the golden arch. She could see Baelon walking down the hill towards the cottages with another new arrival. 'I always feel so sad for the dogs when they walk down the hill towards the cottages for the first time. I know how lost I felt when I arrived. I was so lucky to have Louis waiting for me.'

'Paris was waiting for me too when I arrived,' said Jasmyne.

'Little Fudge came to meet me,' said Meg. 'She is such a thoughtful pup.'

'Olly and the Pupstars are a lovely bunch,' said Lottie. 'They are so supportive of each other.'

'What about you Paris?' asked Jasmyne. 'Who met you when you arrived?'

'Zara took me under her wing and showed me around.'

'Zara and Maisie offer wise council to all,' said Lottie. 'They are such good listeners.'

'It was that spirit of companionship that carried me through the first few months,' said Meg. 'I missed my Mummy so much. I used to sit up here on my own and look across to the arch longingly. I remember the day you found me here Jas and we talked about home. It was so good to share our memories of when we used to meet on the beach with our Mummies. They were such happy times.'

'The best,' agreed Jasmyne.

'And now we're making memories here,' said Paris.

'Time for a group snuggle girls,' said Lottie opening her front paws wide.

The other girls jumped up and they all fell into each other's paws. They held each other tightly and kissed each other's noses. When they finally let go they all had broad smiles.

'We're the Golden Girls,' said Meg, 'and friends for ever!'

*

One More

A Poem by Ian O'Neill

One more hug
One more cuddle
One more stroke
One more snuggle
One more game
One more treat
One more walk
Along our street
One more kiss
One more lick
One more run
One more trick
One more smile
One more bark
One more wag
One more lark
One more fuss
One more beach
One more moment
Within our reach
What would I give for one more …?
… Anything …

Zoe ... A Christmas Story

A Short Story by Ian O'Neill

The Golden gang sat outside their cottages; some chatting, some resting and some looking longingly towards the hill over which the golden arch to the hooman world lay. The day had been full on play; in the forests, in the lake, and in Olly's favourite, the fields of golden barley. But even Olly's batteries needed recharging sometimes. He lay on the lush grass alongside his brothers, Max and Toby, and his latest friend Kevin, whom he'd taken under his wing. Rainbow Bridge was at its most peaceful during these times, a tranquil sea of canine companionship.

Sonny-Boy trotted over to the resting Goldens and sat alongside Max. He sniffed the breeze for a few seconds before laying down in the classic Golden sphinx pose. Max and Toby had become his close friends through the many years they'd all spent together on the Bridge.

'Busy day, Sonny-Boy?' enquired Max.

Sonny looked across at him and smiled. 'It's always a busy day with your little bro around.'

They both nodded. 'Our little bro only has two settings; full on and even fuller on!' said Max.

Olly raised his head and tried his best to look indignant. 'I am here you know. Anyway, I have to keep you old fellas fit.'

'You most certainly do that, little bro,' smiled Toby.

'I've just come from Baelon's cottage,' said Sonny. 'He's about to collect a new arrival.' His gaze turned towards the hillside, and he saw the Elf walking slowly towards the golden arch. 'He was a little subdued. Sad even.'

Olly's ears immediately pricked up. 'Baelon? Sad? Why?'

'The last time I saw him like that was when.' Toby hesitated for a moment, 'was when you arrived here little bro.'

Olly was on his feet in an instant. 'So, it's a young dog he's going to meet. I could help them acclimatise and calm their fears if I went with Baelon.'

'I'm not sure that's a good idea,' said Toby. 'Baelon always greets the new arrivals on his own.'

'I think Toby is right,' agreed Max.

'But I can help!' protested Olly.

Harvey strolled up to them mid conversation. He sensed a little tension in the air. 'Is everything OK?'

'I want to go with Baelon to welcome the new arrival that he's on his way to collect,' said Olly. He looked across to Max and Toby. 'They think it's a young dog and I'm saying that I can help and draw on my experience when I arrived here. If the new dog is anything like I was, they'll be terrified. But Max and Toby don't think it's a good idea.'

Harvey thought for a few moments. 'I think Olly has a point. He has walked this path. You can only ask Baelon, if he doesn't agree, there's no harm done.'

That's all Olly needed to hear and didn't wait for a response. He sped off up the hill after Baelon. He caught up with him just on the brow. The Elf was taken by surprise.

'Olly! What brings you here?'

'The others think you're going to collect a young dog. I can help. I can use my own experiences of how I felt when I arrived here.' He barked the words out in between breaths.

Baelon smiled at him. 'Always thinking of others, young Olly, but I think it would be for the best if I do this on my own.'

'I promise you if the dog gets upset I will back away immediately. Please Baelon, I want to help.'

Baelon looked down towards the golden arch as Daetia and their new arrival stepped through. He watched as the Unicorn talked to the young dog. He turned back towards Olly and saw the anticipation in his eyes. How could he refuse him?

'Very well, Olly, you can come with me, but please be guided by myself and Daetia. This dog is very young, and she needs very careful handling.'

'I won't say anything unless you ask me to,' promised Olly.

Baelon smiled and ruffled Olly's head and they both trotted off together down the hill. Olly was never happier than when he was helping his fellow dogs. He always made a beeline to any new arrivals and loved to show them around, especially through his beloved Fields of Gold. He thought back to that moment he first met Daetia and how he was tempted to run back into the mist, but her love and reassurance persuaded him not to. He was sure he could help this young girl through his own experience.

As he and Baelon approached the Unicorn he saw the young dog looking nervously up at Daetia, confusion clouding her frightened eyes. She looked terrified just as he had been when he first arrived. They stopped a few metres short of the arch and Daetia and the new arrival turned to them. Olly and the young dog studied each other, sniffing the air for each other's scent. Her tail suddenly rose and started to wag.

'Olly?'

Olly for once in his short Rainbow Bridge life was speechless. She seemed to know him. He studied her features carefully. A young Golden Retriever with deep, brown soulful eyes and a pretty smile. Recognition suddenly dawned. 'Zoe?'

Zoe leapt forwards and embraced Olly in her paws. 'Oh Olly, where am I? What's happening to me?'

Olly returned the embrace and stepped back and looked at his friend. 'But how? Have you been ill?'

She shook her head. 'No, one minute I was running out in the open and the next darkness. Then I'm walking through a dense mist where I found Daetia.'

The Unicorn stepped in. 'You were in a tragic accident, Zoe. Your life journey continues. You are on your way to Rainbow Bridge.'

Olly nuzzled Zoe to help reassure her. 'You are safe now, Zoe, I promise you.'

'But what about my Mummy and Daddy ... and Nocas? Will I see them again?'

Daetia lowered her head and looked Zoe directly in the eyes. 'They are always with you, Zoe, in your heart, in your thoughts and in your dreams ... forever. There will come a day when they will all join you here and together you will cross the bridge. But for now, Baelon my Elf friend here, along with Olly, will take you to Rainbow Bridge where you will be safe and looked after.' She kissed Zoe on her head. 'Take care sweet girl.'

Baelon knelt down and stroked Zoe's head. 'Come young Zoe, Olly and I will take you to your new home.'

Zoe looked lost and bewildered. Everything that she had known had been taken in one moment of madness. She looked at them all in turn. The Unicorn was pure white and magnificent and had showered her with love and kindness. Baelon, the Elf, his deep brown eyes were like warm dark pools, his velvet voice soothed and reassured. And then there was her friend, Olly, who she trusted with all her heart.

She snuggled against the Unicorn's legs and gazed up into her bright, shining blue eyes. 'Thank you for looking after me. But there is something I need to ask?'

Daetia smiled. 'Of course, Zoe, anything.'

'Will you look after my Mummy, Daddy and Nocas for me while I'm here?'

Daetia lowered her head and kissed Zoe's ear. 'We will do that together, my sweet girl. Our dreams are always shared with our loved ones, they will never be far away, Zoe, I promise.'

Zoe kissed Daetia's nose and turned to Olly and Baelon. 'I'm ready.'

Together, the three of them slowly walked up the hill towards their home. For Olly and Baelon it was familiar but for Zoe it was all new and slightly frightening. But Rainbow Bridge was made of magic and the love and kindness of that beautiful place were already healing Zoe. And when they reached the brow of the hill, Zoe reacted in the same way as all dogs did when they first set eyes on its beauty.

'Oh my, Olly, it's beautiful.' Tears streamed down her pretty face and off the end of her nose. 'I just wished my Mummy and Daddy and Nocas were here to share this with me.'

Olly nuzzled his head into hers. 'They will one day, Zoe, but until then, me, my bros and my friends will be your family. And let me promise you that you will love them just as I do.'

As they approached the cottages several Goldens walked slowly up to them and Zoe edged closer to Olly for reassurance. Maisie, Zara, Tilly, Maggie and Daisy provided for a gentle and reassuring introduction to her new home.

'Please welcome Zoe to our Golden group,' said Baelon. 'She is a friend of our Olly.'

Maisie stepped forward and nuzzled Zoe. She stepped back and studied her for a second. 'Oh Zoe, you are so young and so pretty. How can life be so cruel to take you away from your Mummy and Daddy at such a young age? Let me promise that we will look after you and that I and the girls here will take you under our wing.'

Each one of them nuzzled Zoe before taking her to one of the cottages and settling her in. Olly looked up at Baelon with sad eyes. 'Was I that frightened when I came here?'

The Elf knelt down and ruffled Olly's head. 'All dogs are frightened when they first arrive, Olly. It is the combination of our care and the love of the dogs that heals you all. And Zoe has you, Olly. I know that you will keep an eye on her and if you have any concerns please come to me or any of the other Elves.'

Over the following days, Zoe's confidence slowly built, and she began to enjoy the new surroundings she found herself in. She ran in the fields, she ran in the forest, she swam in the clear blue lake, and of course, she ran in the Fields of Gold with Olly and his friends. Rainbow Bridge worked its magic as ever.

*

Christmas Eve

As darkness descended, the radiant moon came to rest over the stone bridge casting its luminescent, milky-white glow over the cottages and across the deep, blue lake. Stars glistened in the night-time sky, laughing at the beautiful landscape below. We never ever want to lose our canine children but the thought of them living in such a beautiful place offers enormous comfort. And the care they receive from the Elves and Pixies and each other is second to none.

Every day is awesome at Rainbow Bridge, but Christmas Eve is just that little bit more awesome. The excitement and anticipation about what Santa Paws is going to leave for them in their stockings is electric. And just in case there are any doubts, Santa Paws visits the Bridge every year and each dog has a present. The Bridge is always magical but for these special two days it's just that little bit more magical.

The excitement tingled in the night-time atmosphere as all the Goldie pack were sat outside their cottages. Sonny, Rory, Zoe, Roxy, Hannah, Olly, Max, Toby, Maisie, Zara, Nico, Bob, Rolo, Podge, Jake, Murphy, Harry, Alfie, Ziggy, Chip, Bonnie, Charlie H, Rooney, Charlie S, Bilbo, Honey, Sailor, Maisie H, Annie, Meggie, Molly, Charlie K, Rio W, Charlie H, Rio H, Ava, Willow, Oscar, Megan, Rusty, Champ, Misty, Tilly, Maggie, Daisy, Dexter, Brody, Henry, Ranald, Martha, Ivy, Rumpole, Hitchcock, Harvey, Kevin and their Chocolate Labrador friend, Toffee.

Zoe sat alongside Olly, Max, Toby and Harvey. Her family were never far from her thoughts, but she was slowly coming to terms with her knew life and had settled in well at the Bridge. And she had made some close friendships. There were many more new arrivals after her and she was able to use her experience to help them adjust just like Olly had with her.

Tonight, was a night for reflection for many of them. They sat or lay quietly staring out across the landscape. Peace and tranquillity reigned, and the dogs took the opportunity to relax and enjoy the serenity.

Bob the Retriever had arrived unexpectedly at the Bridge the year before to the day. He had been very ill in the hooman world, and his Daddy had to take the heart-breaking decision to let him go as he hated seeing his boy suffer so much. Bob often thought back to his time at home and how he had loved to sing. His Daddy used to tell him he was a celebrity on this Facebook thing he was a member of. He would film him singing but as soon as Bob realised, he would stop. Singing was all about the love of doing it for Bob not the fame. He loved those times.

And the dogs loved it when he sang. They never knew when he was about to launch into song until he picked up a squeaky ball in his mouth, squeezed it between his jaws to find his pitch and then off he would go. And he didn't disappoint this night because just as he was deciding which song to sing first, one of their friends from the other cottages joined them. He was a brown and white Cocker Spaniel called Ted, or Toothless Ted as the Goldens nicknamed him because his front teeth were missing. And dear Ted inspired Bob's opening song choice.

So Bob's opening song had to be, All I want for Christmas is my Two Front Teeth. And when he came to the chorus, Ted turned to the Goldies and gave them a big gummy smile which caused them all to collapse into fits of laughter and prompted cries of, 'More!'

Now Bob was on a roll and went through his repertoire of songs, including, How Much is that Shoshage in the Window? I'm Dreaming of a Gravy Bone, Barking Around the Christmas Tree, Santa Paws is Coming to Town, Golden Wonderland, Oh Come all ye Goldens, and he finished up with, I Wish you a Merry Christmas!

All the Goldies were on their feet by now barking and laughing. The whole mood had been lifted from one of quiet reflection to one of merriment.

'That's just what we needed,' said Molly, 'it's Christmas Eve so we should all be excited.'

'Look!' cried Zoe. 'She pointed her paw skywards.

'Snow!' Just a few flakes at first but within minutes it was falling as thick as a blanket with the wind swirling it around. The dogs leapt about like lunatics, barking and laughing and some even trying to eat it!

'It's awesome!' shouted Olly.

'It's even better than awesome!' cried Kevin who was by now rolling around in the snow as it settled.

A snowball suddenly splatted into the side of Olly's head showering him in snow. He was momentarily stunned and looked around to see a giggling Pixie running away.

'It's the Pixies!' cried Alfie.

And that was it, mayhem commenced. The dogs ran around like mad things after the Pixies who were throwing snowballs at them. Kevin was right; it was beyond awesome.

The play continued for several hours until their batteries finally ran low, when they all gathered outside the front of their cottages and sat as a group facing towards the golden arch. It was a few minutes before midnight. If there's a better sight in the world than a group of Golden Retrievers sat outside picturesque, thatched cottages on a snow-covered landscape under a moonlit night, I've yet to see it. They were all panting from their exertions, their breath smoking like steam trains in the cold night air.

And then, as twelve o'clock approached, the Elves rang the midnight bells and on the twelfth strike, as a group they said, 'Merry Christmas to all our Mummies and Daddies and to all our families and friends. May peace and love reign over the hooman world!'

And on behalf of all us Mummies and Daddies, may I wish all our furry boys and girls on Rainbow Bridge a very Merry Christmas and a wonderful New Year. Until we meet again.

*

Ballad of Ebenezer Small

A Poem by Jennifer Small

Deck the halls with boughs of holly,
'Tis the season to be jolly;
'Bah humbug' quoth Ebenezer Small
From his chilly turret in Runrig Hall.

'For all this Christmas festivity,
I've not the slightest proclivity;
Ho bloody ho to Yuletide joy,
It wasn't like this when I was a boy.

We huddled round a fire of Polton peat,
Wondering if there'd be enough to eat;
From a single crust we ate our fill
While Father toiled at t'paper mill.

A mutton bone was our Christmas feast
A relic of some ancient Highland beast;
A mouldy swede, a bowl of gruel
Was all we had for our festive Yule.'

Thus Ebenezer sat and reminisced,
Supping from a pot of vintage Scotch mist,
When suddenly a blinding glare
Flashed through the dank and dusty air.

Ebenezer's heart beat with sudden fright
(Had someone switched on an extra light?)
And then he saw amidst the gloom
A great Golden dog, shining in the room.

The Apparition glowed like molten Gold,
A fearful sight for mortal man to behold;
Then smoothing down its rippling hair,
It parked itself in the nearest chair.

Poor Ebenezer sat as still as marble stone,
Wondering whether to bribe it with a bone,
When the Apparition raised a furry paw,
And pointing, said 'Ebenezer, you're a bore!

I'm the Ghost of merry Christmas Tide
And this night with Rudolph I've hitched a ride;
You're in dire need of some seasonal jollity,
Mistletoe, crackers and general frivolity.'

So saying, the Ghost waved its feathery tail
And conjured up a bucket of steaming ale;
Two woofs produced a bottle of sherry,
Three mince pies and a pudding with a holly berry.

Next appeared a tall green fir tree
All decked with lights blazing merrily;
'Who'll pay my electricity bill!' Ebenezer wailed
But the Ghost just grinned as Ebenezer quailed.

'Now all we need' said the Ghost 'is a turkey' –
At which Ebenezer began to feel rather perky –
One bark brought a brown and juicy bird,
Two, a duck and a goose, the third.

The Ghost sat back as pleased as Punch
Surrounded by this gargantuan brunch;
But Ebenezer Small, no smile could he raise
As he saw the Yule log all cheerily ablaze.

The Ghost tapped its claws, less than elated
To find its efforts so unappreciated;
But Ebenezer cried 'I'm such a monstrous beast,
I've no-one to share my Christmas feast!'

'No problem' said the Ghost, 'that I can fix,
I've still a few things left in my box of tricks;
And scratching its floppy ear with its paw
It pointed to the window by the door.

Shivering in the bitter winter wind they stood
Poor waifs, waiting for a crumb, a scrap of food,
Frozen snouts pressed longingly against the pane,
The queue stretched all along the snowy lane.

There was Theo and Pearl, Coopy, Mully and Lexie
And Ted and the Mattos girls looking oh so sexy,
With Bramley and Bailey, Barney, Brax and Mae
And Gracie, Loki, Duffy and Samson ready to play.

Handsome Freddie had Princess Kim on his paw
Followed by Lottie and Teal, fur sparkling with hoar,
There were the Island Girls, Ben, Indy and Rosie too
Not forgetting Bill, Charlie, Murphy, Rosco and Roo.

'Poor things! Let them come in' Ebenezer cried,
'They can warm themselves by my fireside!
I'll share with them all my Christmas banquet
'Cos we have meat and save the Lord be thankit!'

But the Great Retriever (for it was he) espied
That Ebenezer was still quite unsatisfied;
On his face was no sign of festive cheer,
Gloomily he sighed 'Something's missing here'

The Great Retriever showed his fangs in a grin
And said to Ebenezer 'Go and let the others in,
They're not forgotten, of that you can be sure
So why don't you go and open up the door?'

So Ebenezer did what he'd been told to do
And saw before him a sea of Gold of every hue,
Wagging their tails they flowed past in a stream,
A Golden carpet, shining all a-gleam.

There was Paddy Byrne leading the spectral crew
Followed by Murphy O'Neill, his number two;
Finlay Cuddlemonster was arm in arm with Tilly,
He still had an eye for a pretty little filly!

Along came Bruce, no more aches or pain,
Frolicking with Meg just like a pup again,
Cassie & Teddy, Hardy, Molly, Roxy and Belle,
Ellie Mae and others too many to tell.

Said the Great Retriever 'On every Christmas Eve
The gate to the Bridge I open for those who grieve,
And through the snow and ice and frost
Home they come, all those we've loved and lost.'

Now each year at Christmas tide
The gate at the Bridge is flung open wide
And a flood of those who've gone before
Beats a path to Ebenezer's door.

And so ends this tale of Ebenezer Small
Who once lived all alone in Runrig Hall;
Now no more in his dreams does he roam
To days of yore in his comfortless home;

Thanks to that ghostly spectral hound
For joviality Ebenezer's now renowned;
He whose views were once so cynical
Of Christmas cheer is now the very pinnacle!

Pearl's Christmas Ballad

A Poem by Jennifer Small

It's Christmas Eve at ancient Runrig Hall
But Ebenezer's not expecting carolers to call,
He's huddled crouched over a dying ember
Waiting for the end of a miserable December.

You'll find no Christmas spirit in this old pile,
No-one's laughed or joked here for quite a while,
There's just dust and cobwebs and musty gloom,
And overall, a sense of pervading doom.

But hark! What noise is through the sleet and hail?
A pitiful whine, a pathetic sobbing wail,
And as Ebenezer peers out into the driving rain
He sees a face pressed up against the windowpane.

Now Ebenezer doesn't like visitors to Runrig Hall,
In fact, no-one's welcome there at all;
And as he angrily throws open the door,
Poor soaking Pearly-woofer lifts a pleading paw.

'Oh please, kind Sir, I've just escaped from the pound,
And it'll be the chop for me if I'm found,
I'm cold and wet and my feet are sore,
I just can't walk a single step more.

She fixed him with tearful big brown eyes
And Ebenezer, to my and your surprise
Took pity on this bedraggled waif and stray –
Perhaps it was the effect of Christmas Day?

In she came and cowered in a corner her teeth all a-chatter
Till Ebenezer snarled 'Now what's the matter?'
'I'm just so hungry' Pearl whimpered with a moan
And so Ebenezer threw her a half-chewed bone.

Suddenly the walls of that crumbling pile began to shake
And to the door Ebenezer fled fearing an earthquake.
But no! It was the Great Retriever in all his splendour
Guardian of the breed and Pearl's stout defender.

In he strode shaking starlight from his glowing fur
And to Ebenezer he snarled 'You miserable cur',
His fangs gleamed as he rumbled with a growl
'How dare you treat one of my children in a way so foul?'

Now Pearl gazed up at him quite mesmerized
Bewitched by that Golden face and wise brown eyes,
'You poor wee smout' he tenderly crooned
And Pearl rolled on her back and swooned.

If you think Ebenezer's troubles are over and done,
You're wrong, they've only just begun;
What's that ominous tapping at the oaken door?
It's Bill Badger scratching with a mud-encrusted claw.

'Evening Squire', he said, his beady eyes gleaming bright
'Any chance of putting up a badger for the night?
And a bit of dinner would go down a treat
The ground's so hard I can't find a single worm to eat.'

So saying, across the threshold Bill Badger shuffled
By his lack of welcome quite unruffled;
Pearl in her corner gave out a friendly bark
And Ebenezer muttered 'It's looking a lot like Noah's Ark'.

'My larder's bare, it's quite empty' said Ebenezer with a wail
But such feeble excuses could in no way prevail,
And as the cupboard opened he began to shake
For there inside was a turkey, a tin of Chum and a Xmas cake.

Alas, it was just as Ebenezer feared
Before his eyes his hoard of goodies disappeared,
Rubbing his furry paws together with a smile
Said the Great Retriever 'This'll keep us going for a while.'

The tin of Chum went in the badger's bowl
And Pearl got a turkey and stuffing roll,
Then sitting round the fire they got quite merry
Drinking Ebenezer's bottle of sweet sherry.

But all good gatherings must come to a close
And at length to his paws the Great Retriever rose,
'Time for me' he woofed 'to be on my way'
I promised to help Santa to unload the sleigh'.

'It's a shame to break up this little party,
But you know how it is, things to do, places to be';
Then to Ebenezer he growled 'Never you fear –
I'll be back to check on you lot next year'.

And as his tail disappeared round the door
In his wake he left a pile of presents galore;
Pearl got a smart new coat for when the winds were keen
And Bill Badger perpetual rights to dig the Runrig Hall demesne.

'But what of old Ebenezer?' I hear you say,
'What did the Great Retriever leave him on Christmas Day?'
Now Ebenezer was the most blessed of the three
For he was gifted with a ready-made family.

Bill Badger's sprawled out on the floor
His furry bulk reverberating with each snore,
And Pearly-woofer (who's now no half-starved scrap)
Is curled up comfortably on Ebenezer's lap.

Now Ebenezer's life is changed beyond our ken
And he's really quite the happiest of men;
No more a crotchety curmudgeon full of bile
They come from countries far for the warmth of his smile.

The doors of his mansion are open to all
And Runrig Hall's a refuge for creatures great and small;
You'll be pleased to know that even Ebenezer has to agree
Life's much better when you've got friends for company!

Another Ballad of Ebenezer Small

A Poem by Jennifer Small

'Twas the night before Christmas and Ebenezer Small
Was throwing a party at Runrig Hall;
For drinks and food he was footing the bill –
Old Ebenezer's changed since he lived at Polton Mill.

All the world and his wife had been invited
And they'd all accepted, quite delighted;
In they streamed, all manner of folks
While Pearl took their hats and coats.

Good King Wenceslas was there with his page
And the ghosts of Christmas present and future age,
While Christmas past lurked to steal a mistletoe kiss
From any pretty girl who stopped to reminisce.

Snow White came with her followers, all seven –
The Ugly Sisters thought just one would be heaven –
And Cinderella and her Prince waltzed round the room
'Cos they were still on their honeymoon.

Sir Paddy Byrne dispensed mulled wine and Xmas cheer
While Max Emillion and Asbofreddie poured out the beer;
Rosco was test-tasting each festive nibble
And agreed they're much better than his usual kibble.

Annie & Misty were floozying round the floor
Wiggling their fluffy bits and waving a flirty paw;
Who needs bunches of holly and mistletoe
When the Mattos girls are putting on a show!

Overhead the Herald Angels played their harps,
Plucking out the neutrals, flats and sharps,
And the Good Christian Men with one voice
Cried out to one and all 'Rejoice!'

Now Ebenezer gazed around with pride,
With his soiree he was well-satisfied,
But pride they say goes before a fall
And so it was with Ebenezer's ball.

What's that? The sound of angry drumming hoofs
Tearing across Runrig Hall's ancient roofs!
A crash! The old oak doors opened wide
And a deathly chill fell on those inside.

There stood an icy figure glittering with snow,
Icicles hanging from every finger and toe,
Frost-rimed hair streaming in the arctic blast –
The guests gazed at this awful sight aghast.

'Where's my invitation?' the dreadful spectre screeched
And Ebenezer froze, his face all white-bleached,
How could he have forgotten the White Witch?
But she'd come anyway – ain't life a bitch!

By Ebenezer's snub the Witch was not at all amused
Her status, she felt, had been sore abused;
So, waving her wand, she turned the company to stone,
Cackling 'I bet you wish you'd stayed at home!'

With that into her chariot she lightly stepped
And cracking her whip, her horses forward leapt,
Trailing ice and rime and hoary frost
Until to human sight she was quite lost.

Now, gentle reader, do not be dejected,
There's one by this disaster not affected,
Young Pearl had gone for a midnight stroll
Searching for the odd unwanted sausage roll.

Back to Runrig Hall she trod the snowy path.
Looking forward to the blazing hearth,
And with a rather chilly, furry paw
Pushed open the creaking door.

At that dreadful sight a lesser dog would quail
But a retriever's courage is never known to fail,
So, uttering a faint and piteous moan,
She dialled a number into her mobile phone.

To Santa she called with extreme urgency,
Saying 'Come quick, this is an emergency!
I'm really sorry to be such a pain
But Ebenezer's got himself in trouble again'.

Said Santa 'Sorry, dear, I'm already in my sleigh,
You know I'm on double time until Christmas Day,
But don't worry, I've someone in the vicinity
Who'll sort it out just as well as me.

I left him somewhere up near Cassiopea,
So he'll be with you in a trice, never fear,
Just stand outside and give a bark
And he'll know where to come in the dark'.

So Pearl sat woofing in the freezing air,
When, suddenly, appeared in a blinding glare,
An Apparition most fearful to behold,
A Great Retriever glowing like molten Gold.

'Right' It said, 'Santa sent me at the double,
What seems, young Pearly, to be the trouble?
Old Ebenezer got himself into a fix?
Somebody here been playing nasty tricks?'

With that, he strode into the Hall
Where ice and snow lay like a shrouded pall,
And shivering in the wintry chill,
Said 'Didn't Ebenezer pay the heating bill?'

With a flourish of a furry spectral paw,
The Hound slammed shut the open door,
'A quick warm-up is all you require
Plus an extra knob of coal on the fire'.

So saying, he waved his feathery tail
And hot wind blew like a tropic gale,
Melting ice dripped from Ebenezer's nose
As all the stony figures slowly unfroze.

Soon the Yule log was merrily ablaze
And all the company sang the Great Retriever's praise,
Truth to tell, he was secretly elated
To find his efforts so much appreciated!

But all good things must come to a close
And at midnight up the Great Retriever rose,
'With the Christmas Fairy I've got a date
And it wouldn't do for me to be late'.

His glowing shape began to shine and shimmer
And faded to a Golden glimmer,
But his words echoed through Runrig Hall,
As he barked 'Take my advice, Ebenezer Small!

In future, double check your guest list
Just to see there's no-one that you've missed,
And when you next throw a celebration
Make sure I also get an invitation!'

A Rescue Retriever's Letter to Santa Paws

A Poem by Jennifer Small

Santa, wait! Do you perhaps remember me?
I'm the retriever rescued from a life of misery;
I've tried so hard to be a good girl all the year
So you'd bring me a pressie for my Christmas cheer.

I deserve something nice, I really think I do
Could you find me a turkey leg or maybe two?
A new Staghorn wouldn't go to waste,
The one I've got has lost all its taste.

If I ask nicely will you put under the tree
A small selection of goodies just for me?
Gravy biscuits and a big, meaty bone
Something to chew when I'm home alone.

But hark! a little voice has whispered in my ear
And I agree entirely with what I hear,
To ask for anything would just be greed
Because I've got everything that a dog could need.

No more will I be left in the sleet and rain,
Tethered in the yard at the end of a chain,
Wondering what it was I did wrong today
To make them treat me in this way.

Never again will I cower shaking on the floor
Waiting for a slap or a kick or more,
Trembling in fear for the beating to come,
Lying there, terrified and dumb.

I won't be thrown out in the bitter cold
Just because I'm getting old,
Left to starve and die in the icy winter street,
The skin ripped from my sore and frozen feet.

Never again will my name be uttered with a curse
As I'm beaten, tormented and worse;
Is today the day that I'll get some dinner?
Or will I lie here ribs protruding, getting ever thinner?

Never again will I be thrown outside the door,
Left for days because I'm an unwanted chore,
Knowing that it's my fate to shiver here in pain,
Knowing that all my love has been wasted and in vain.

Now I've got a Mum who loves me beyond all measure,
Who cuddles me and call me her little treasure,
And when she lifts her hand to touch my head
I know that it won't be a slap but a caress instead.

I've got a warm soft bed that's all my very own,
I'm safe there when I want to be alone,
And at bedtime I snuggle up to my Mum so tight
So she can stroke me if I wake up scared at night.

My dinner bowl is filled up twice a day
With proper food not scraps to be thrown away,
I go for walks and meet my friends in the park
And no-one shouts or hits me when I bark.

I've got a blankie and a basket of toys of every design
I've never had so many things that I can call mine;
But what's best of all, I've got a family of my own
And I'm here to stay in my forever home.

And when at last to Rainbow Bridge I make my way
To find my friends and in green meadows to play,
My final journey I won't be alone or afraid to face
'Cos I'll be cradled in my Mum's loving embrace.

So dear Santa, keep my presents in your sack,
There's nothing you can give me that I lack;
Let them all go with my love instead
To some poor dog with nowhere to lay his head.

There's just one wish I have left, a heartfelt plea
And it's that all dogs are loved just as much as me.

A Puppy Christmas

A Short Story by Ian O'Neill

It's Christmas Eve. Every day is special on Rainbow Bridge. But Christmas Eve is even more special. Every dog, no matter how old, gets excited at the prospect of Santa Paws bringing them presents. Maisie sat alongside Zara, Sonny-Boy and Harvey watching the three puppies play on the grass. They played only the way puppies can play. Running, rolling, nipping, and lots and lots of joyful yapping.

'I never tire of it,' said Harvey.

'Me too,' said Sonny. 'You're doing a fine job, Maisie.'

'We all are,' said Maisie. 'Every Golden on Rainbow Bridge loves these three. We are all parents to them.'

Cody came running up. 'Mummy Maisie, when is Olly coming back from the Fields of Gold. He'll play a chase game with us.'

'He'll be back soon enough, little one,' said Maisie.

'Why can't we go to the Fields of Gold with him and the Pupstars?'

Maisie smiled. 'You're too little – you'll get lost.'

'But Bambi, Little Sausage and me can run really fast.'

Harvey and Sonny smiled together. 'When you're a little bigger, Sonny and I will take you there, I promise. And you can all play chase games,' said Harvey.

The words were no sooner out of his mouth when Olly ran down the hill with his Pupstars hot on his trail. When he saw the puppies playing he ran over and skidded to a halt in front of them.

Cody and Bambi screeched, 'Olly!' while Little Sausage ran round and round in circles joyfully yapping.

'Right then, who wants to play bitey face?' he asked and ran around them barking and wagging his tail. The three puppies yapped with excitement and chased him all over the grass until he lay on his back, and they crawled all over him, playfully nipping his ears and ruff. Zoe, Buddy, Kevin, Fudge, Holly and Doris joined in, and Goldie chaos broke out.

'Olly and the Pupstars are so good with them,' smiled Maisie.

'I could do with some of their energy,' laughed Harvey.

The supper gong sounded, and the play instantly stopped, and they all ran into the cottages, happily barking at the Elves for their food. As the bowls were placed on the floor, the barking stopped like a switch had been flipped. Bowls were licked furiously, tags jingling against the tin, followed by the slurps of water and contented burps. A scene every Goldie owner has witnessed many times.

Bambi, Cody and Little Sausage immediately surrounded Maisie. 'Can we go out and play with Olly and the Pupstars?' asked Cody.

Maisie shook her head. 'You need to rest after your meal. Give your food an hour to digest and then you can play before you go to bed.'

'Oh but, Mummy Maisie we want to play,' pleaded Bambi.

Maisie gave them her look that they instantly knew and the three of them reluctantly retired to their beds and let out a collective sigh as they lay down.

*

The Goldies sat outside the cottages enjoying a cold, crisp Christmas Eve evening. A full moon glowed like a giant ball in a star-filled sky. It was a night to fill your hearts with joy and even more so as the puppies played with Olly and his friends.

'I've always loved Christmas,' said Dougal.

'Me too,' agreed Podge.

'Do you remember Dad always shared his bacon sarnie with us on Christmas morning,' said Rory turning to Sonny.

'I do indeed,' said Sonny.

'I loved tearing the wrapping paper off the presents,'

said Podge.

'Me too agreed,' Harry.

'And the Christmas dinners were awesome,' said Rumpole.

'I'd always get some turkey on my dinner and delicious gravy,' said Jake.

'And the shoshages wrapped in bacon,' chimed in Podge.

They all laughed. 'A shoshage always makes it for you, Podge,' laughed Harvey.

Little Sausage had broken away from the playing and had been watching the adults chat, and out of the blue said, 'Shoshage!'

Maisie eyes opened wide, and she said, 'Did you hear that? His first word!'

She ran over and snuggled him. 'Oh little one, that makes me so happy.'

Podge was delighted that shoshage was his first word. 'So you're Little Shoshage.'

And he repeated, 'Little Shoshage.'

The playing pups stopped and ran over to him. 'Little Shoshage it is then,' laughed Olly.

'What we need now is a song,' suggested Toby. 'Come on Bob, you've always got a song on your lips.'

Now, those of you who know our Bob, also know that he doesn't need much encouragement when it comes to singing. He barked and cleared his throat and started. It was a Christmas song familiar to us all. But maybe not the words we are used to!

'On the first day of Christmas my Mummy gave to me,
A prime shoshage in a sar-ni,
On the second day of Christmas my Mummy gave to me,
Two Bonios and a prime shoshage in a sar-ni,
On the third day of Christmas my Mummy gave to me,
Three meaty snacks, two Bonios and a prime shoshage in a sar-ni,
On the fourth day of Christmas my Mummy gave to me,
Four squeaky toys, three meaty snacks, two Bonios and

a prime shoshage in a sar-ni,

On the fifth day of Christmas my Mummy gave to me,

Five rubber rings! Four squeaky toys, three meaty snacks, two Bonios and a prime shoshage in a sar-ni,

On the sixth day of Christmas, my Mummy gave to me,

Six tennis balls, five rubber rings! Four squeaky toys, three meaty snacks, two Bonios and a prime shoshage in a sar-ni,

On the seventh day of Christmas, my Mummy gave to me,

Seven tuggy ropes, six tennis balls, five rubber rings! Four squeaky toys, three meaty snacks, two Bonios and a prime shoshage in a sar-ni,

On the eighth day of Christmas, my Mummy gave to me,

Eight nylabones, seven tuggy ropes, six tennis balls, five rubber rings! Four squeaky toys, three meaty treats, two Bonios and a prime shoshage in a sar-ni,

On the ninth day of Christmas, my Mummy gave to me,

Nine furry toys, eight nylabones, seven tuggy ropes, six tennis balls, five rubber rings! Four squeaky toys, three meaty treats, two Bonios and a prime shoshage in a sar-ni,

On the tenth day of Christmas, my Mummy gave to me,

Ten forest walks, nine furry toys, eight nylabones, seven tuggy ropes, six tennis balls, five rubber rings! Four squeaky toys, three meaty treats, two Bonios and a prime shoshage in a sar-ni,

On the eleventh day of Christmas, my Mummy gave to me,

Eleven yoghurt pots, ten forest walks, nine furry toys, eight nylabones, seven tuggy ropes, six tennis balls, five rubber rings! Four squeaky toys, three meaty treats, two Bonios and a prime shoshage in a sar-ni,

On the twelfth day of Christmas, my Mummy gave to me, twelve filled kongs, eleven yoghurt pots, ten forest walks, nine furry toys, eight nylabones, seven tuggy ropes, six tennis balls, five rubber rings! Four squeaky toys, three meaty treats, two Bonios and a prime shoshage in a sar-ni …!'

Every dog joined in the last verse and when they finished they all jumped up and down, barking and wagging their tails in appreciation. The atmosphere at that moment was wonderful. Just describing it brings a lump to my throat. The three puppies joined in the revelry, but it was getting late, and Maisie wanted to settle them down to bed.

'Come on puppies, time for bed.'

'Oh, Mummy Maisie,' pleaded Cody and Bambi, 'just five more minutes.'

'You need to be fresh for tomorrow for when Santa Paws comes.'

They were just about to argue when someone shouted, 'look, it's snowing!'

Just a few flakes at first but within seconds it became a heavy blanket and started to settle.

Sonny turned to Maisie and smiled. 'I don't think there's any chance they will sleep now.'

Maisie knew he was right. 'Very well, you can play in the snow for a little while and then bed.'

The three pups rushed up and kissed her nose before running off into the falling snow with the others. It was Goldie play at its best with the pups running and rolling in the snow with the bigger dogs barking their delight. The Pixies made an appearance, and they threw snowballs in the air for the dogs to try and catch before turning it into a massive snowball fight.

As midnight approached, tiredness set in and the Goldies prepared themselves to return to their cottages for their final treat of the day and a well-deserved rest. Cody, Bambi and Little Sausage had almost run themselves to sleep and lay on Maisie and Zara struggling to keep their eyes open.

'Come, little ones,' said Maisie, 'it really is time for your bed,' and she received no protests this time.

But then Maggie suddenly called out. 'I can hear bells.'

A hushed silence fell on the Goldies as they all listened intently. And sure enough they could hear the faint sound of bells. They looked towards the hill in front of the cottages and peered through the falling snow. A tingle of anticipation ran through every one of them as they watched and waited.

And then, as if by magic, they saw a sledge being pulled by six reindeer on top of the hill heading towards them. And the cry rang out.

'It's Santa Paws!'

An aura of sheer joy and love surrounded Santa's sleigh. The reindeer trotted in perfect coordination; their proud antler heads held high. Now you would've thought that the dogs would have gone wild with excitement, but they stood in respectful, or was it stunned, silence. Santa Paws had never made an appearance in front of them all before. Some claimed to have heard his sleigh bells in the night and others said they had seen him.

But this? This was a whole new experience. Santa's sleigh slowly but carefully ploughed a path through them and stopped outside the cottages. He tethered the reins and stood up and looked all around him.

'And a Merry Christmas to you all!'

The dogs all sat down staring at Santa in awe. Fudge was right next to the sleigh looking up at him with stars in her eyes.

'Is it really you, Santa Paws?

Santa let out a huge, 'Ho Ho Ho!' his trademark laugh, and stepped down from the sleigh.

'Oh, little Fudge, you are growing up so fast.' He reached into his sack in the back of his sleigh and handed her a gift-wrapped package. 'Merry Christmas to you little one.'

Fudge looked up at him, tears glistened her eyes. 'Is that from my Mummy?'

Santa knelt and hugged her. 'It comes with your Mummy's love, little Fudge.'

Fudge jumped up and kissed Santa's thick, white bushy beard and said, 'Thank-you, Santa.' He placed the present into her mouth and she took a step backwards, so the others could take their turn.

'So,' said Santa, 'where are those three little puppies?' He looked across to the cottage where the three little ones were sitting with their Mummy Maisie. Each one in turn looked up to Maisie and then back at Santa.

'Come little ones, I have presents for you all.'

'Go on,' encouraged Maisie, 'go and see Santa.'

They all seemed a little overwhelmed by the situation, but Cody led them over to Santa's sleigh and he crouched down and gave them a collective hug. 'I've heard all about you from the Elves. I hear your Mummy Maisie is doing a fine job looking after you.' He looked across to her and smiled. 'So, time for your presents.' He stood up and reached into his sack and took out three gifts wrapped in silver paper and tied with bows. He handed one to each of them with a hearty, 'Merry Christmas!' Cody, Bambi, and Little Sausage all hugged him with their little paws before running back to Maisie.

'Come,' said Santa, 'don't be shy, I have presents for you all.'

The dogs all went up to Santa one at a time until each of them held their gifts in their mouths. Olly looked to his friends and then his brothers before dropping his on the floor. He had a question.

'Er, Santa Paws?'

Santa turned to him and stroked his head. 'Yes Olly, how can I help you?'

'Can we open our presents now?'

Santa let out his huge trademark laugh again. 'Of course you can! After all, it's Christmas!' He jumped back up into his sleigh, took the reins and shouted, 'A very Merry Christmas to you all! And now I must carry on delivering the presents to the rest of Rainbow Bridge.' He sat down and called out, 'Lead on, Rudolph!' And off they went as every Golden Retriever went about ripping off the wrapping paper from their presents.

*

Maisie lay on the veranda outside the cottage. She was joined by Maggie, Murphy, Dougal, Harvey, Toby, Max and Sonny and Rory. They stared out onto a sea of wrapping paper strewn across the snow. It was the calm after the storm following the mass unwrapping of the presents.

'Well, I've had some awesome Christmas Eves since I've been on the Bridge but that was the best ever,' said Sonny.

'Absolutely,' agreed Rory.

'Little Sausage fell asleep with his Mini-Kong still in his mouth,' said Maisie. 'All the cream cheese filling was gone though,' she laughed.

'Wasn't it wonderful to see the puppies having such fun,' said Maggie.

'Olly was in great form,' said Max. 'He loves playing with the puppies.'

'And they love playing with him,' said Harvey.

'Although I miss home,' said Dougal, 'I've had the best time tonight. I mean, seeing Santa Paws.'

They all nodded their agreement.

'Wouldn't it be wonderful if we could let our Mummies and Daddies know about tonight,' said Maisie.

'But we can,' said Murphy. 'The Chronicler will let them know.'

'Of course,' agreed Maggie. 'Baelon told me he walks among us.'

'He knows my Mummy,' said Murphy proudly.

Sonny and Rory exchanged knowing looks. 'Everybody knows him, but nobody knows him,' said Sonny mysteriously.

'So why don't we send a message home from us all,' suggested Toby.

'We could send it from every Golden Retriever on Rainbow Bridge to every Mummy and Daddy in the hooman world,' said Maisie.

'Do you think the Chronicler will hear us?' asked Maggie.

'I have a feeling he might,' said Rory smiling at his brother.

All nine Goldens stood up and looked across towards the

golden arch. Harvey led them in their Christmas wishes. 'Sending all Mummies and Daddies back home a Christmas wish from every Golden Retriever on Rainbow Bridge. Have a wonderful Christmas and remember, we're waiting, we're always waiting. Merry Christmas!'

*

I Still Walk Beside You

A Poem by Dave Gravestock

I still walk beside you
Just lighter than before
No more tippy tappy claw
No more scratches on the floor
But when you blow your whistle
So high you cannot hear
I'll raise my head, twitch my nose
And I'll cock my crooked ear

You won't see me coming
But I've seen you have cried
So I'll come a racing
To be there by your side
And I'll always walk beside you
Just lighter than before

I was always there for you
You were always there for me
Don't worry that I've gone now
I've found a favourite tree
And I'll always walk beside you
Just lighter than before

We walked the lanes, the beaches,
the parks and the hills
We got sunburnt, blown inside out
And had so many other thrills
As I always walk beside you
Now lighter than before

Don't hang up my collar, lead
Use it for a new little wag
Meet up with all the old crew
Please treasure just my tag
I'll be there walking beside you
Just so much lighter than before

I'll make room for your new love
You know what I mean
I'll visit when you least expect
When I pop up in your dream
I'll be laying there beside you
Just lighter than before

One day, come and walk with me
No rush to cross that bridge
But when the time is right
We will walk the rainbow ridge
And once more we'll walk together
Just lighter than before.

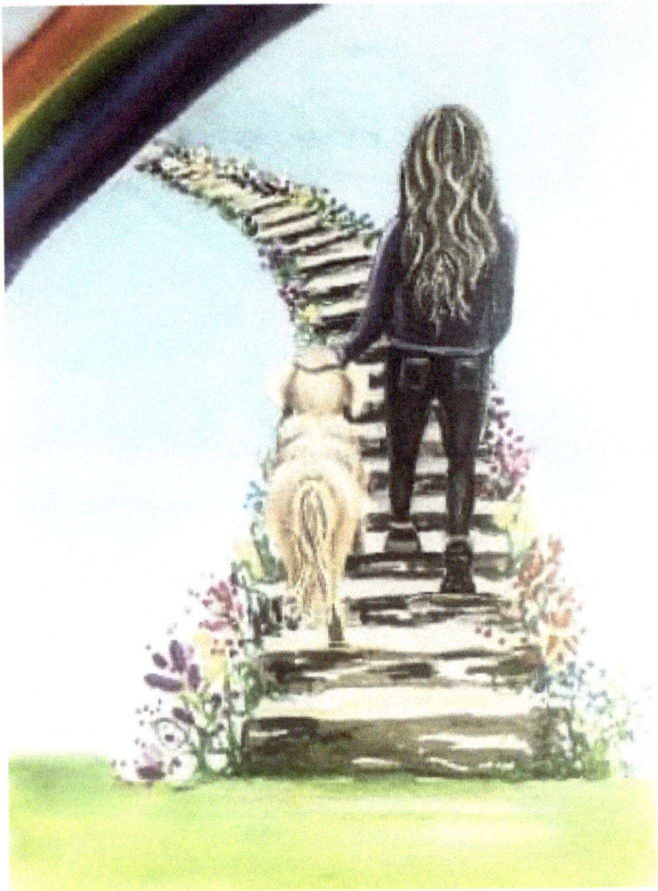